P9-BIE-601

Who Will Win the Lifeguard of Love?

"Give me a break, Tamera," Tia said. "You'd do anything to get Patrick away from me, wouldn't you, even steal from your own sister."

"How can I get Patrick away from you when he was never with you, huh?" Tamera demanded. "You're just a sore loser because Patrick thinks I'm fun and he likes me better."

"How can he ever have a chance to know if he likes me if you're always butting in, acting like a total idiot, and stealing my ideas?" Tia yelled.

"You know what your problem is, don't you?" Tamera began.

"Stay away from me. I'm not talking to you anymore," Tia muttered, and she started to walk away.

"Two can play that game, Tia Landry," Tamera called after her. "I'm not talking to you, either."

Sister Sister

☀ SUMMER ☀ DAZE

JANET QUIN-HARKIN

A MINSTREL® BOOK

Published by POCKET BOOKS
New York   London   Toronto   Sydney   Tokyo   Singapore

A MINSTREL PAPERBACK *Original*

 A Minstrel Book published by
POCKET BOOKS, a division of Simon & Schuster Inc.
1230 Avenue of the Americas, New York, NY 10020

Copyright © 1997 by Paramount Pictures

ISBN: 0-671-00287-2

First Minstrel Books printing August 1997

10 9 8 7 6 5 4 3 2 1

A MINSTREL BOOK and colophon are registered trademarks of Simon & Schuster Inc.

Printed in the U.S.A.

Chapter 1

❧❧

I can't wait to get out of this place!" Tamera Campbell exclaimed as she flopped down at the table in the cafeteria beside her friends Michelle, Chantal, Sarah, and Denise. "Do you know how long I've been standing in line, just because I forgot to bring my lunch today? And I was surrounded by creepy little freshman boys making dumb jokes and trying to push each other into me. And when I got to the food counter, all they had left was this!" She held up a dried-up slice of pizza, curled at the edges with one piece of shriveled pepperoni clinging to it. "Can you believe it? Two bucks for this? They should pay me to eat it."

"Hang in there, girlfriend," Michelle said. "Only two more weeks to go and then we're out of here."

"I don't think I can survive two more weeks,"

Tamera said. "Is it just me, or does this year feel like it's been going on forever and ever?"

"It's not just you," Sarah said. "I'm crossing off the days on my calendar at home."

"I would be too if I were going to Hawaii this summer," Denise said. "You are so lucky, Sarah."

Sarah shrugged. "Is it my fault that I've got a rich aunt who doesn't have any children of her own, and I'm so adorable that she just has to take me everywhere with her?"

"Shut up," Chantal said, giving her a friendly push that almost sent her off the bench into a passing group of boys.

"I know you're crazy about me, but you don't have to throw yourself at my feet," one of the boys said, grinning at Sarah's embarrassment.

"Euwww—get me out of this place," Sarah muttered as she attacked her yogurt again. "Those two weeks can't go fast enough for me."

"I just hope I'm out of this place for the summer," Tamera said. "I'm scared to death I'm going to flunk a class and have to take summer school."

"They're not making me take summer school," Michelle said. "I'm just going to flat-out refuse. I've already got my ticket to go visit my grandma in Florida again, and nothing's going to make me stay in Detroit this summer, Principal Vernon included."

Tamera looked up to see the bad-tempered principal heading toward their table. Principal Vernon sure had a knack for showing up where he wasn't wanted, she thought. She nudged Michelle to shut up.

"What?" Michelle demanded. Then she saw the principal. "Whoops," she muttered.

Tamera held her breath as the principal passed them.

"Phew, that was close," Tamera said.

"Two more weeks and I'll have forgotten he exists, when I'm lounging on those white sand beaches in Florida," Michelle said.

"And I'll be hanging ten on those waves in Hawaii," Sarah added.

"Just what is hanging ten?" Denise demanded.

Sarah shrugged. "I'm not sure, but it's what you do when you're in Hawaii. I'll let you know when I get back."

"You guys are so lucky," Tamera said. "How come I don't seem to have any useful relatives in great vacation spots?"

"Talking of relatives, where's Tia?" Denise asked.

"Science club meeting," Tamera said.

"Better her than me," Chantal said, grinning at Tamera.

"Me, too," Tamera said. "I can't understand how anybody would want to do science when they don't have to. But you know Tia—she actually likes stuff like that."

"That's weird, because she seems so normal otherwise," Michelle said. "I mean, she likes hanging out at the mall with us and going to movies and flirting with guys just like we do."

"Oh, there she is now," Tamera said as she spotted her twin sister, Tia Landry, coming into the cafeteria.

"I guess the science club meeting must have gotten out early. Can we squeeze her in here?"

"Oh, she's got that geeky girl Heather with her," Chantal muttered. "We don't want her at the table with us. She'll tell us how we shouldn't be eating meat and how paper plates are destroying trees."

"I take back what I said about Tia being like us," Michelle said. "I don't know what she can see in that Heather girl. She gives me the creeps."

"Me, too," Tamera said. "I spent the night at her house once. Her room is like the science museum. She has planets on her ceiling and a giant telescope and an iguana! I was totally freaked out."

The other girls looked at each other in disgust.

"How come you and Tia are twins and yet you've turned out so different?" Denise asked.

Tamera shrugged. "I ask myself that all the time. I don't think it's fair that she got all the brains, for one thing. Sometimes it feels like we're from different planets. I'm praying that I pass my classes and don't have to take summer school. Tia is actually applying to take a summer program for high school kids at Detroit University."

"She wants to study over vacation?" Michelle asked. "She's even weirder than I thought."

"Tell me about it," Tamera said. She stopped talking as Tia arrived at their table, with the serious-looking Heather behind her, wearing a plaid skirt and white shirt, her long, dark braid hanging down her back.

"Is there room for two more?" Tia asked.

"I guess," Chantal said. "Scoot over, Tamera."

"There are no empty seats in this whole place," Tia said, squeezing in next to her sister.

"Is it my imagination, or are there more kids in this school than there were last September?" Michelle asked.

"Maybe they clone freshmen in your science club," Tamera said, looking at her sister with a challenging grin.

"Oh no, scientific ethics would never allow the cloning of humans," Heather said, before Tia could answer. "But very interesting experiments are being done with animals right now."

Tamera caught Michelle's glance. Michelle put her finger in her mouth and pretended to gag. Tamera grinned.

"Is that what you're going to be doing in your summer school at the university, Tia?" Michelle teased.

"That would be cool," Tia said. "Anyway, I don't even know if I've been accepted yet. They only take a few high school students, and I'm not even going to be a senior."

"Of course you'll be accepted," Tamera said. "You came in third in the citywide science fair. Are you telling me they'll only take two students?"

Tia smiled modestly. "I just don't want to get my hopes up too high," she said. "I need to get a scholarship, too, or I can't afford to go."

"You'll get it, Tia," Denise said warmly.

"I hope so," Tia said. "It would be great to see

what science classes are like at the university. I might get to watch some real research. Wouldn't that be fantastic?"

"I might be working in a real science lab this summer," Heather said with enthusiasm. "My dad teaches at Wayne State, and he's going to try to get me a lab assistant's position. Then I'd actually be taking part in real research."

"Gee, Heather, that sounds like fun," Tia said.

"Yeah, a total blast," Tamera added sarcastically, making Tia kick her under the table.

"At least we plan to be occupied for the summer," Tia aid, frowning at Tamera. "I haven't heard too much about your plans yet."

"I plan to be occupied, too," Tamera said. "I'm getting the perfect job, and I'm planning to make tons of money and then go on the world's biggest shopping spree."

"What is this job, Tamera?" Sarah asked excitedly. "How come you didn't tell us about it?"

"Because I haven't found it yet," Tamera said. "I was thinking of starting my job hunt this weekend."

"Good luck," Chantal said. "I've been trying to find a summer job for weeks now. It seems like all the good jobs get snapped up by college students."

"You guys could always come and work with me," Denise said.

"Doing what?" Tamera asked.

"My cousin runs this nature camp for city kids. It's really neat. They bus kids out from the city to this wildlife preserve and teach them all about nature.

I promised my cousin I'd be a counselor this summer, and now I'm really looking forward to it. I love working with little kids." She turned to Tamera. "I think they're still looking for counselors if you're interested."

Tamera shrugged. "I don't know much about little kids, and I know nothing at all about nature," she said. "Tia will tell you the only thing I could identify on my science final was a flower petal."

"I don't know much about nature either," Denise said, "but there's counselor training before we start. Come on, Tamera. It would be fun if you did it, too."

"I don't think so, thanks," Tamera said. "You're used to little kids—I'm not. I've never even baby-sat. I tried it once and was grossed out when I had to change a diaper."

"The kids aren't that little," Denise said. "They're between seven and ten. No diapers. And my cousin said we're going to be doing a lot of fun stuff. The camp is right on the shore of Lake Erie, and they have canoes and campfires—all the things we used to do in Girl Scouts."

"Correction—*you* used to do in Girl Scouts. I was never a Girl Scout."

"You weren't? I thought you joined when we all did, back in fourth grade."

Tamera shook her head. "I joined for one week. I flunked knot tying, and then I dropped out. Remember, I tied my knot to the door handle and they had to cut us out of the room?"

"And you're totally clueless in the great outdoors,"

Tia added. "Remember that time you took my place at the day camp and you got lost on a field trip?"

"So? It was wilderness. I admit I don't have wilderness skills. It could have happened to anybody."

"It was a park with a nature trail next to the freeway, Tamera. And you got me fired from my job, remember?"

There was a tense silence, then Heather said brightly, "I used to love being a Girl Scout. I got so many badges that they had to give me a second sash."

Tamera caught Michelle's eye and started to giggle. Tia kicked her again under the table.

"I really don't think it matters if you don't have outdoor skills, Tamera," Denise said hastily, before Tamera choked into her milk. "We'd just be junior counselors. We wouldn't have to plan the activities, and think of all the hunky lifeguards we could meet at the lake."

"Hunky lifeguards, huh?" Tamera's face lit up. "Maybe I could learn to like a job that had guys in cute little Speedos as one of the perks. What's the pay like?"

"Not great," Denise said. "Minimum wage."

"Forget it," Tamera said. "I plan to get rich this summer. I need a whole new wardrobe for the fall. I have to come back as a fashionable upper-class person. And I'd like to throw out my bedroom furniture and totally redecorate. Oh, and I'm planning to buy my own car when I get my license."

"Tamera, I don't think they have summer jobs as brain surgeons or movie stars," Tia said. "Face it, you're not going to make that much money. People don't pay kids much."

"Just you wait and see," Tamera said. "I'm going to convince somebody that I'm so mature and talented that they'll pay me real money."

"To do what?" Tia demanded.

"The sort of thing I'm good at—meeting the public, selling things—anything that makes use of my dazzling personality."

"Dream on," Tia said.

"Hey, it doesn't hurt to dream," Tamera said.

"I'm already dreaming about the guys I'm going to meet on the beach in Waikiki," Sarah said.

"Shut up," everyone said in unison this time.

"I'm so jealous," Chantal said. "How come there are no hunks in Detroit?"

"I'm sure there are—they just don't go to this school," Michelle said.

"I told you, they're all at this nature camp," Denise said.

"Yeah, right." Michelle laughed. "They'll probably turn out to be wimpy little guys who carry around binoculars and tell you they've just spotted the lesser black-throated night crawler."

"Bird-watching is one of my hobbies," Heather said.

"It figures," Chantal muttered under her breath to Tamera.

"Guy watching is one of my hobbies," Tamera said. "Maybe I'll borrow my dad's binoculars and come visit your camp, Denise."

"I guess you must have gotten over your last boy-friend, Tamera," Denise said.

"You're right. I'm ready for a fun and exciting summer."

"Me, too," Tia added.

"Maybe you'll find a cute lab assistant at your summer program," Tamera said with a grin to Michelle.

"And if you found one, you could clone him for Heather," Michelle added.

"I thought I explained that the process of cloning—" Heather began.

"Chill, Heather. They were only teasing," Tia said quickly.

"I wonder if guys ever feel like they're dating clones when they go out on double dates with you guys," Sarah said thoughtfully.

"No way," Tamera said. "Nobody could mix up my fun-loving, witty personality with my quiet, serious sister."

"Give me a break, Tamera," Tia said. "You make me sound like a geek. I can be noisy and fun loving too if I want to."

"Oh, sure. Your idea of fun loving is a trip to the library."

"It is not!" Tia said.

"Which of us dates the serious guys and which of us attracts the gorgeous, muscled hunks?" Tamera demanded.

"Was somebody just talking about me?" a voice said in Tamera's ear. She spun around to see her neighbor Roger standing behind her, his dreadlocks dancing as he bent his head toward her.

"Roger, what are you doing snooping on other people's conversations?" Tamera demanded.

"That's the way you hear the most interesting things," Roger said, grinning delightedly at her. "I was just thinking about you, my little flower, and remembering the last blissful date we had together."

"Roger, I went out with you once because I felt sorry for you," Tamera said.

"But then you were captivated by my magnetic personality," Roger said, "and you had the time of your life—admit it."

"I did not."

"Then how come you said you'd had an evening to remember?"

"Because I wanted to remember never to repeat it," Tamera said. "Now, get lost, please. You're putting me off my food."

Roger beamed at the other girls around the table. "She's really crazy about me," he said. "She just has a hard time expressing it in public."

"Roger, go away!" Tamera yelled, making half the cafeteria look up.

Roger went on grinning. "It's okay, I can wait. We've got the whole summer ahead of us. We can spend all those lazy, hazy, crazy days together, hanging out in your backyard, with you wearing your cute little bikini . . . and all those summer nights, sitting on my porch, watching the moon, my strong arm around your delicate shoulder. . . ."

He wandered away, leaving Tamera making a horrified face.

"What were you saying about all the gorgeous hunks who followed you around?" Tia asked with a triumphant smile on her face.

Tamera shot a worried look at her sister. "Now I definitely have to get a job for the summer—a job with long, long hours, preferably far away. I have to be busy every minute of the day and night, or I'll get stuck with Roger!"

Chapter 2

⚲

*H*ey, Tia, get down here," Tamera called as she picked up the mail the next Saturday morning. "You've got a letter."

Tia came running down the stairs, pulling on her robe. "From Paul?" she asked, still hoping to hear from her former boyfriend.

"No, from the University of Detroit."

"Ohmygosh." Tia snatched the envelope from Tamera. "This will be it, Tamera. Now I'll know whether I've been accepted into the program."

She ripped open the envelope. " 'Dear Ms. Landry. We are happy to inform you'—They're happy, Tamera. It must be good news. 'We're happy to inform you that you have been accepted into the summer science program for gifted high school students.' " Tia dropped the letter and grabbed Tamera, whirling her around excitedly. "I'm in, Tamera. They've accepted me!"

"That's great, Tia," Tamera said with a forced smile. She was still finding it hard to imagine how anyone could be excited about doing extra science classes all summer.

"And listen to this, Tamera," Tia went on. " 'We are also pleased to offer you a scholarship to help you meet the tuition costs.' " She looked up at Tamera again, her eyes shining with happiness. " 'The amount of your scholarship is fifty dollars.' "

"How much is the tuition?" Tamera asked.

"Eight hundred," Tia said flatly.

"Eight hundred dollars?" Tamera shrieked. "Where are you going to find eight hundred dollars, Tia?"

"I'm not," Tia said, slumping onto the nearest sofa. "There's no way my mom could come up with that kind of money. When they said they offered scholarships, I thought it would be for the whole amount, not a crummy fifty dollars."

She sat there, staring out across the room. Tamera went to sit on the arm of the sofa beside her. "Does that mean you can't go?" she asked cautiously.

"What do you think?" Tia snapped.

"Maybe my dad could lend you the money and you could pay him back," Tamera suggested.

"Oh, sure," Tia said bitterly. "If I'm going to school all day, how would I have time to get a job to pay him back?"

"I thought maybe your mother . . ." Tamera started to say, then she didn't finish the sentence.

They both knew that Tia's mother hardly made enough money from her fashion designs.

Tamera got up. "Maybe if I get my dream job, I'll earn enough to help you out," she said.

Tia got to her feet and stood, staring at Tamera. "That is so sweet of you, Tamera," she said. "Sometimes you're the world's nicest sister. But I couldn't take your money, even if you did make enough to lend me. You need it for yourself."

"I guess your education is more important than new clothes for me," Tamera said.

"My mom could always design you some," Tia said, smiling again now.

"Sure, thanks a lot," Tamera said. "I want to be in fashion, not in trouble!"

"She tries hard," Tia said. "And she really wants the best for me. It's not her fault that she's not very good at fashion designing. That's why I kept quiet about this summer program."

"You didn't tell your mom you were applying for it?"

Tia shook her head. "I decided not to mention it unless I knew I could get a scholarship. I knew she'd only try extra hard to sell her dresses and it would stress her out." She waved the letter as she walked across the room. "Lucky I didn't tell her, huh?"

Tamera watched her sister, feeling angry and helpless. It didn't seem fair that Tia couldn't go when she studied so hard all year.

"I bet my dad would help out if he knew," she said.

Tia spun around. "You'd better not tell him, Tamera. Your dad has already done enough for us. Promise me you won't tell him."

"Okay," Tamera said.

"I can handle it," Tia said. "It's not like it's the end of the world or something. Now I'll just have to go job hunting with you. Maybe we can get glamour jobs together."

"Let's go job hunting today," Tamera said. "Come on, go get dressed, and then we'll take the world by storm."

"What did you say about taking the world by storm?" Tia asked as they made their way slowly up the street toward their house. "I feel like I've been hit by a tornado. Do you know how many miles we must have walked today? How many buses we've ridden? How many times we've had our feet stepped on?"

"And all for nothing, too," Tamera said. "I can't believe there's no job for us in the whole city of Detroit."

"Apart from Rocket Burger," Tia said. "They said they'd be happy to have us back."

"I'd rather die first," Tamera said. She pushed open the front door and staggered inside.

"Where have you girls been all day? Shopping again?" Tamera's father, Ray Campbell, asked, looking up from a baseball game on the TV.

"They look like they've been in a fight," Tia's mother, Lisa Landry, said suspiciously as she appeared from the kitchen. "They can't have been shopping. It's not even super sale day."

"We've been out hunting for summer jobs," Tamera said, sinking onto the sofa beside her father.

"And we've walked miles and miles," Tia said.

"Any luck?" Lisa asked.

"Nothing," Tamera said. "And everybody was so rude to us, too. They almost shoved us out of the door and told us to get lost."

"Well, you did have a nerve, Tamera," Tia said, "going into that TV station and telling them you'd like to be the weather girl for the summer."

"I don't see why they said I had to have a meteorology degree first," Tamera said frostily. "I know how to point at maps."

"I'm not surprised you didn't come up with a job if you had such big ideas, Tamera," Ray said. "Kids have to start off at the bottom, working their way up, just like I did."

"Oh yeah, we know all about your childhood when you were so poor that you had to walk barefoot to school," Tamera said, grinning at Tia. "You've told us a million times."

"I got my first job washing cars," Ray said. "And now look at me. I own my own limo company. Don't be afraid to do hard work, young lady. It's good for you. In fact, if you're interested in washing cars this summer, then I could use you."

"Uh—thanks all the same, but I'd rather not, Dad," Tamera said. "I don't want to wind up with dishpan hands."

"So where else did you girls try?" Lisa asked. "Did you ask at the mall?"

"That was one of the first places we tried," Tia said. "And there was nothing except for Wiener Express."

"What's wrong with Wiener Express?" Ray asked.

Tia gave Tamera a quick glance.

"Dad, you don't work in fast food when you're our age," Tamera said. "That's okay for a first job, but we couldn't let our friends from school see us working there. Have you seen what their uniforms are like? Talk about geeky."

"It seems to me that you girls are being too choosy," Ray said. "A job is a job."

"We want it to be fun, too," Tamera said, "And we don't want to work for minimum wage."

"You girls could always come and help me," Lisa said. "I'd give you a job."

"You would? Doing what?" Tia asked, giving Tamera a worried look.

"Helping me run the fashion cart," Lisa said. "One of you could attract customers by modeling the clothes, and the other could watch the till. It would give me more time to work on my designs. I'd give you ten percent of everything that you sell."

"But, Mom, you hardly sell anything," Tia said. "Tamera and I want to make money this summer."

"But thanks for the offer, Lisa," Tamera said hurriedly. "It's nice to know that one of our parents is trying to help us out." She wrapped her arms around her father's neck. "Don't you know somebody who could help us, Dad? You drive all kinds of famous people around. Don't you know a rock star who would like a personal assistant for the summer?"

"If I did, I wouldn't recommend you," Ray said, laughing.

"Why not? I'd be a great assistant."

"Tamera, assistants need to be organized. I wouldn't call a person who forgets to turn in half her homework assignments organized. And another thing, I don't want my daughter mixed up with rock stars."

"Oh, come on, Ray, don't be such an old fuddy-duddy," Lisa said. "What's the good of mixing with the rich and famous if you can't pull strings for your own child?"

"Lisa, I only chauffeur the rich and famous sometimes. It's not as though I belong to the country club with them."

"Don't you know anybody, Ray?" Tia asked. "Heather's father is helping her get a job in a lab at the university."

"I'll ask around," Ray said. "But I can't promise anything."

The doorbell rang.

"If that's Roger, I've gone on an Antarctic expedition until September," Tamera called as Tia headed to the door.

She opened it. "Oh, it's you, Heather," she said, making a face at Tia. "Come on in."

Heather followed her shyly into the room.

"Hi, Heather, what's up?" Tia asked, coming to

meet her. "You remember Heather, don't you, Mom? Ray?"

"Yeah, you're the brainy one with the creepy reptiles in the bedroom, right?" Lisa said.

"Mom!" Tia wailed in despair. "Don't mind my mother, Heather," she said rapidly. "She loves to tease."

"I just stopped by to see if you'd heard yet," Heather went on brightly. "Some other kids I know got letters today."

"Heard what?" Lisa and Ray asked at the same time.

"From the university," Heather said at the same time as Tia said, "Nothing."

"Oh yeah, the university," Tia said loudly. "They were sending out brochures to kids who might want to apply there later. I got one, but I don't think I'm interested."

"Brochures? What are you talking about?" Heather asked. "I meant the program—"

"Oh yes, they do have an interesting degree program, but it's too far in the future for me to think about yet," Tia babbled on. "Are you hungry, Heather? I was just about to fix myself a snack. Let's make one together, right?" She grabbed Heather's arm and swept her toward the kitchen.

"Wait, but I don't want a snack," Heather protested.

"Sure you do," Tia said.

"Why are you acting so weird, Tia?" Heather asked as the kitchen door swung shut behind her.

"Because I haven't told my mother about the program at the university," Tia whispered. "I got my letter today, and they accepted me."

"So why aren't you telling anybody? I'd want everyone to know if that was me."

"Because they only gave me a tiny scholarship, and I can't afford to go," Tia said bluntly.

"Oh, I see." Heather's face fell. "Gee, I'm sorry, Tia. You were looking forward to that so much. It's a pity it wasn't at Wayne State, or I could have asked my dad to see what he could do for you."

"It's okay," Tia said. "The big problem is that I was kind of counting on it. Now I have to find something else to do with my summer. Tamera and I were out job hunting all day and we came up with nothing. There are no jobs out there for teenagers."

"I could ask my dad if you could come work with me as a lab assistant," Heather said.

"You could?"

"Sure. I bet they could use someone smart like you."

"Wow, Heather, that would be terrific," Tia said.

"It would be fun working together, wouldn't it?" Heather said, looking excited, too. "Maybe we'd be in the lab when they came up with some great new discovery."

"It would be almost as good as doing my summer program," Tia said. "Do you think there's really a chance they'll take me?"

"My dad thinks you're very smart," Heather said. "I'm sure he'll do what he can."

"I've been feeling so depressed all day," Tia said. "Now I'm so excited. Working in a science lab for the summer would be my dream job."

"Let's go over to my house right now and ask him," Heather said.

Tia burst out of the kitchen. "Mom, I'm going over to Heather's house to see if her father can get me a job at the university!" she yelled.

Suddenly she felt excited and hopeful again. A job at the university, working in a real science lab—she couldn't think of a better way to spend her summer!

Chapter 3

෨

"*T*amera! Where are you? Listen to this!" Tia's voice echoed through the house.

Tamera looked up from the *Brady Bunch* rerun she was watching.

"What is it?" she asked.

Tia came into the room, her face shining with happiness. "Guess what? Heather just called me, and her dad has arranged it. I'm going to be working with her at the university lab. Isn't that amazing?"

"Oh yeah, totally amazing," Tamera said.

"You don't sound very happy for me," Tia said.

"Tia, I'll try to be happy for you, but frankly, the last place on earth I'd want to work is with geeky scientists, surrounded by germs. Just don't bring samples of your work home in your pockets. I really don't want the plague this summer."

23

Tia laughed. "You are funny," she said. "Not all science labs work with germs. Heather says they're doing research into calcium-binding proteins and amino acids."

"Oh, that sounds fascinating," Tamera said dryly. "But I already know how to bind my proteins when I smush my egg and my bacon together."

Tia laughed. "Ha ha," she said. "I'm talking about the actual structure of cells. This is big stuff, Tamera. I might be part of a cure for cancer or diabetes. And working with Heather will be fun, too."

"Oh yeah, a barrel of laughs," Tamera said.

"And you know another good thing," Tia said. "I won't have to go out and buy new clothes for work."

"Because you're among geeks?"

"No, because everyone has to wear a white lab coat. I'll get to feel like a doctor. I wonder if mine will have my name on the pocket."

"Aren't you kind of letting this go to your head?" Tamera asked. "You don't think they'll let you do any real work there, do you? You don't have all those degrees you need to bind up your proteins, or whatever it is they do."

"They might let me help out with the simple things," Tia said, "like taking readings and making charts."

"Oh, I get it. All the fun stuff," Tamera said.

"Well, at least it's better than Rocket Burger or Wiener Express. They're the best you've come up with so far."

"I'm working on it," Tamera said. "I'm waiting

until school gets out. Then I can really put all my energy into hunting for the perfect job. I know it's out there. Now all I have to do is find it."

On the last day of school, Tia, Tamera, and their friends sat outside, eating their lunches in the shade.

"See, the weather turned perfect in time for the summer vacation," Michelle said, gazing up at the clear, blue sky.

"It's going to be like this every day in Hawaii," Sarah said.

"Shut up!" all the girls said at the same time. They laughed and threw napkins as Sarah ducked.

"That will be the one bad thing about working in a lab," Tia said. "I won't have a chance to enjoy the summer."

"I offered you a chance to be outdoors every day," Denise said. "I'm going to end the vacation fit and healthy from all that fresh air and lake water."

"Denise, nobody gets fit and healthy from contact with Lake Erie," Tia said, laughing. "When I'm in the lab, I'll analyze a sample for you. You'll freak out when you see what's swimming around in there."

"I heard they'd done a great job cleaning it up," Denise said. "And anyway, it's going to be fun. I think getting paid for canoeing and swimming is great."

"You forgot to mention the little kids," Tamera said. "You'll be busy keeping an eye on zillions of little kids and making sure they don't drown while they go canoeing and swimming. It's not the same thing at all."

"You still don't have a job, Tamera?" Chantal asked.

Tamera shook her head. "I'm going to start hitting the employment services tomorrow," she said. "I'm sure I could be a great receptionist or personal assistant."

"It's funny, isn't it," Tia said thoughtfully. "This is the first summer when we're all doing something more than goofing off by the pool or the lake. I guess this is what grown-up life is going to be like."

"If I don't find the perfect job, I'll get to goof off," Tamera said. "That might not be such a bad idea after all—a lounge chair in the shade in the backyard, sprinkler to cool me off, boom box beside me, trashy book to read or the portable TV outside, dish of ice cream . . . Yeah, I could live with that!"

When Tamera woke the next morning, she wondered why it was so bright. She sat up and looked at the clock. Eight-thirty!

"Tia, wake up!" she yelled. "The alarm didn't go off."

"Are you crazy?" Tia growled from under the bedclothes. "It's vacation. We don't have to get up."

"Oh, right," Tamera said, feeling foolish and annoyed. She got out of bed. "It's a perfect day out there," she said. "Great pool weather. Want to go to the neighborhood pool with me?"

"Sorry. I promised Heather we'd get ready for

work next week," Tia said. "We want to read up on what they're doing in the lab, so that we can be intelligent and helpful. And I thought you were going job hunting?"

"Maybe tomorrow," Tamera said. "Today is my unwinding day. I'm going to take the lounge chair under the tree and watch all the morning shows on my dad's little TV."

As soon as Tia had gone to Heather's house, Tamera put on her white lace bikini and covered herself with sunscreen. She told herself that she was the lucky one if she got to spend the summer like this. She told herself that there was no way she'd want a job like Tia's, but she couldn't put the nagging jealous feelings from her mind. How come Tia always got the good stuff? People always said, Tia, you're so smart, and offered her good things. Now Tia would be making money and Tamera would have nothing to spend on clothes or treats. And she really didn't want to work in a fast food place again. That would be too embarrassing!

I'll find something, she told herself. I'll go out there and find the perfect job, and I'll have the most fun summer. But first, it's goofing-off day!

She took her father's portable TV and all the snacks she could find, then she pulled the lounge chair into the shade of the big maple tree in the backyard. Ray walked past his bedroom window, looked out, and saw her. He came outside. "Tamera, what are you doing?" he asked.

"Enjoying my summer vacation," Tamera said.

"I thought you were going to find a job."

"When the weather turns cloudy," Tamera said. "Right now I'm making the most of summer."

"At least you could be starting on your summer reading list," Ray said.

"Are you serious? This is the first day of vacation, Dad. Give me a break. I'm supposed to be relaxing after an exhausting school year."

"Exhausting school year," Ray said with a despairing grin. "Someday you're going to have to learn about hard work, young lady."

Tamera watched him walk back into the house, then she went back to her TV show. She was enjoying a program about people who thought they were vampires when a loud roaring noise made her jump out of her skin.

She sat up in alarm as her father's big power mower came charging right at her, with grass flying in all directions. She scrambled to lift her feet onto the chair as the mower passed her by inches. It was only then that she recognized who was driving the mower.

"Roger! What are you doing?" she screamed.

Roger switched the mower down to idle. "Sorry, my little flower. I didn't mean to startle you. I haven't quite gotten the hang of this thing yet. It's one powerful sucker, and I'm not exactly the world's strongest man."

"You can say that again," Tamera said, cautiously uncurling her legs. "But to repeat my question—what are you doing with my dad's mower?"

"Your father is paying me five bucks to mow his lawn," Roger said. "I suggested it when I knew that you'd be out here in your bikini every day. Actually, I should be paying him five bucks to be alone with you like this. I've never had the chance to keep you trapped in one place before. I'm going to mow around and around in a circle until you and I are there, together, in the middle, imprisoned in our own private world of love."

"In your dreams, Roger," Tamera said, hastily gathering her TV set and her snacks before she fled back to the house.

"Hey, it's bad luck to walk over new-mown grass!" Roger called after her, but she kept on running.

"Dad?" she yelled, then stalked through to Ray's study. "Why did you tell Roger he could mow the lawn?"

"I thought the boy was being enterprising, Tamera," Ray said. "He is actively going after work, as you should be doing. He's finding a need and filling it."

"Yeah, and his need is to bug me," Tamera said. "How can I relax in the backyard if Roger and his mower keep swooping around me, missing my toes by inches?"

"You could go find yourself a job, like Roger," Ray said.

"You gave him a job," Tamera said. "You didn't offer it to me. And Heather's father got his daughter a job. Even Lisa offered us work, although there was no way she'd ever be able to pay us. How come you don't even want to help your own daughter?"

"Of course I want to help you, Tamera," Ray said, "but I don't see what I can do."

"Every time someone hires your limo, you could ask him if they have a job for your daughter."

"I suppose I could," Ray said. "If I could be sure of one thing."

"What's that?"

"That you'd really work hard and stick at it, Tamera," Ray said. "I wouldn't want to go out on a limb for you and then find that you were goofing off and not doing a good job."

"I'd do a good job, if you found me something fun to do," Tamera said. She wrapped her arms around his neck, which usually worked when she wanted something badly. "I promise, Daddy. I wouldn't let you down."

"Okay, I'll see what I can do," Ray said.

Tamera kissed him on the cheek. "Thank you, Dad. You're the best father in the world," she said. "I know you'll find me a great job and I'll earn enough money to buy all my own clothes and you won't even have to give me an allowance."

Ray laughed. "I'll believe that when I see it," he said.

Chapter 4

ᦒ

"Tamera, I've found you a job," Ray called as he came home the next evening.

"You have?" Tamera came flying down the stairs from her room. "What is it? Am I going to like it?"

"I think so. It's with a radio station that you seem to listen to all the time."

"Not Happenin' Radio?" Tamera shrieked.

"Is that what it's called? It's WBBQ."

"That's it! WBBQ! Happenin' Radio. 'We're so sharp, we're on the cutting edge!'" Tamera yelled in a radio DJ voice. "Dad, you're incredible. How did you manage it?"

"I had to give a ride to the station manager—"

"Was Beastman in the car, too?"

"Beastman?"

"He's their famous deejay. Beastman and Leopard

Lady. They have the evening show that everyone listens to."

"There was no Beastman in the car," Ray said. "And if I'd known you'd be working with beastmen and leopard ladies, then I wouldn't have been so eager to get you a job there. I never thought to ask what kind of music they played. You know I don't like music about gangs and violence, Tamera."

"Relax, Dad," Tamera said. "They play all the latest stuff, cool but not weird. All the kids at school listen to it." As she said this, a wonderful picture came into her head—Tamera on the air with Beastman, making jokes for all of Detroit to hear. And when she met someone from school she could say, "Did you hear me on Happenin' Radio last night?" and they'd be green with envy.

"So, uh, exactly what will I be doing, Dad?" she asked.

"Anything they need help with, I imagine," Ray said.

"Cool," Tamera said. She pictured herself helping to write the scripts, choosing the music, maybe even filling in for Beastman while he went on a break. "Dad, you are definitely the coolest. Who knows, maybe you've started me off on the road to stardom."

"Just as long as you have a productive summer and you learn to be reliable and hardworking, that's all I care about, Tamera."

"Did they say when I could start?"

"Tomorrow. I said I'd drive you down there in the morning. After that, you have to take the bus."

"Tomorrow?" Ohmygosh, I don't have anything to wear. I'll have to go to the mall this very minute. I don't suppose you'd drive me, would you, Dad?"

"I just got home, Tamera, and I'm back at work tonight," Ray said. "One of my drivers is sick, so I have to drive a limo myself. Besides, you have a closet full of clothes."

"Yeah, but nothing right for working with Beast-man," Tamera said. "My clothes are all little-girl, goody-two-shoes stuff. I need something mature and sexy."

"You are not going out of this house looking mature and sexy," Ray said.

"At least let me go buy a new outfit," Tamera said. "New clothes are good for a person's self-esteem, you know. And I'll be too shy to do my best at work if I'm wearing crummy old clothes."

"I'm not stopping you from buying a new outfit, Tamera," Ray said. "Just get something suitable for your age."

"There is one thing stopping me from getting a new outfit," Tamera said. "Money. I don't suppose you could advance me fifty dollars on my salary, could you?"

"You know I don't like lending you money, Tamera," Ray said.

"Did I hear that child say she needed a new outfit?" Lisa asked, coming through from the kitchen with a slice of cold pizza in her hand. "I just came down to get myself a snack and I couldn't help overhearing when I put my ear to the door."

"I've got a job at my favorite radio station, Lisa," Tamera said. "I'm so excited, but I really need something new to wear."

"No problem, honey," Lisa said. "I'll design you something and run it up tonight. And you don't even have to pay me. When the people at that radio station admire it, you can tell them it's a Lisa Landry creation." She headed back for the kitchen. "I'd better get started right away," she said. "It should make a bold statement. Spandex, I think—orange and black, or maybe red with a splash of purple."

"Dad!" Tamera wailed.

Ray reached into his pocket. "Okay, here's fifty dollars," he said quickly. "I can't have you going to work looking like a spandex bumblebee."

Tamera reached up to kiss him. "Thanks, Dad, you won't regret it," she said. "I wish Tia would hurry up and get home. I want her to come shopping with me."

Tamera waited impatiently until Tia walked in with Heather around six o'clock.

"We've had a very productive day at the library," Heather said. "I think we can safely say that we've made ourselves familiar with calcium-binding proteins, wouldn't you, Tia?"

"I'll say," Tia said. "I read so many articles on microfilm that my eyes won't focus anymore. I think I'd better go take a nap."

"You can't take a nap," Tamera said, grabbing her arm. "You have to come shopping with me for a new outfit."

"Tamera, a new outfit can wait until tomorrow."

"No, it can't," Tamera said, "because it's a work outfit and I start work tomorrow."

"You do?" Tia grinned happily. "You found a job that wasn't Rocket Burger?"

"You'd better believe it," Tamera said. "How about production assistant at Happenin' Radio."

"Oh yeah, right," Tia said, laughing. "Dream on."

"No, seriously, it's true. My dad gave a ride to the station manager and told him about me. I start work tomorrow."

"Tamera!" Tia screamed. "I am so excited for you. It's the perfect job, just like you said. You're right, we have to go shopping right now. You want to come, Heather?"

Tamera was shaking her head and mouthing No! No! behind Heather's back. Luckily Heather shook her head, too. "No thanks. I really have to get all these notes on the computer right away. But have fun, you two. I hope you find a nice new dress."

"What planet is Heather from anyway?" Tamera asked as she and Tia left the house together. "A 'nice new dress' for a radio station? Give me a break."

"It's just because she's been brought up by two science professors," Tia said. "She can't help it if no one at her house ever went to the mall."

"Never went to the mall?" Tamera shrieked.

"Well, maybe when she needs a new notebook or shoes," Tia said. "She doesn't hang out like us."

Tamera made a face. "Sometimes I wonder how

you can stand to be around her, Tia. Doesn't she bug you?"

"Occasionally," Tia said, "but she knows so much. It's neat to have someone smart to talk to. Most people think I'm weird or showing off if I want to talk about anything other than boys or shopping or movies. It's going to be great, working with a whole lot of smart people."

"Now I'm glad you got all the brains," Tamera said, "or I might have been going to some lab tomorrow, instead of going to work with the Beastman himself."

As they walked through the mall, they saw Michelle, Sarah, Chantal, and Denise sitting in the food court, eating ice cream.

"Hey, Tia, Tamera, come and join us," Michelle called. "They've got a new flavor. Udderly Delicious—made with extra cream."

"Sorry, we can't stop right now," Tamera said. "I start my new job tomorrow, and I have to find the right outfit to make a good first impression."

"You found a job? All right!" Sarah said. "Where are you working?"

"WBBQ," Tamera said.

"The Happenin' Radio station? With Beastman?" Michelle shrieked so loudly that half the mall turned around to listen.

Tamera nodded. "My dad helped me get a job as production assistant," she said. "I'll probably be helping to choose the music, write the dialogue—that sort of stuff."

"Wow, Tamera. I am really impressed," Chantal said. "Will you get me Beastman's autograph?"

"I'd be happy to."

"Hey, do you know Beastman?" a boy asked as he walked by with his friends.

"She's going to work at the radio station this summer," Tia said.

Pretty soon Tamera was surrounded by a big group of kids, all asking for Beastman and Leopard Lady autographs.

"I'll do my best," Tamera said. "They might not want to sign all these."

"Tell Beastman we're his biggest fans," one of the boys said. "We hang out here at the mall all the time so you'll have no problem finding us."

"And maybe by the end of summer, you'll be asking for my autograph, too," Tamera said. "I'm hoping I'll get my chance on the air, you know."

"Really?" The crowd of kids looked impressed.

"Are you going to be Kitten Lady?" one of the boys asked.

Tamera grinned. "Who knows?" she said smoothly.

She looked around and almost had to pinch herself. She was the one who had stood quietly while Tia picked up all kinds of awards and got written up in local papers, and now finally she was the famous one. It felt great!

Chapter 5

❧❧

*F*or once Tamera got up super early and spent hours getting ready. She put on her new seventies zigzag-print shirt with her yellow denim miniskirt and finished the outfit with her new clompy white vinyl boots. Then she swept her hair up into a ponytail. She wanted to look fashionable but efficient—the kind of assistant the people at the station could trust with important things.

"You look just right," Tia said as she watched Tamera put the finishing touches to her hair. "Now I kind of wish I wasn't stuck wearing this old lab coat all summer," she went on. "But if I'm going to be a doctor or a scientist someday, then I guess I'll have to get used to wearing one."

"Maybe your mother will design you one in purple and orange," Tamera teased, then she grew serious again. "I hope she wasn't too offended when I showed her the clothes I bought and told her I didn't need her spandex outfit today."

"I think you should have told her you didn't need it—ever," Tia said. "She's still making it, you know. She'll want you to wear it sometime at the station."

"I'll wait until they all love me there and then I can wear what I like," Tamera said.

"I hope it goes well for you, Tamera," Tia said. "I think it's great that you're doing something you really love. Who knows, maybe this will help you to decide on a future college major and career."

"Yeah, who knows," Tamera said. "But I don't see that you need to go to college at all to become Beastman or Leopard Lady."

"You wouldn't really want to be someone like that, would you?" Tia looked worried.

"I might," Tamera said. "Okay, I'm ready. Wish me luck. And tune in to 'Live ninety-nine point five.' Who knows, you might hear me on the air!"

"Wish me luck, too," Tia said. "You might be looking at a future Nobel prize–winner about to make her first scientific breakthrough!"

"Ready for your big day?" Ray asked as he stopped the car outside the building where a big WBBQ Happenin' Radio sign was flashing.

"You'd better believe it," Tamera said. "I really want to succeed in this, Dad. I'm going to work super hard and make you proud of me."

"That's my girl," Ray said, smiling at her affectionately. "Remember what I've taught you. Give one hundred percent all the time and you can't go wrong."

"Okay, Dad," Tamera said. She got out and gazed up at the flashing neon sign. "Here goes nothing!" She gave him what she hoped was a confident wave and ran into the building.

Tamera's heart was beating so loudly that she was sure everyone could hear it as she waited by the reception desk for the program manager to come for her.

At last a tall, skinny guy with shoulder-length hair came running into the foyer. He didn't seem to be much older than Tamera. He looked around with a worried expression, then saw her sitting in one of the armchairs.

"You must be the new assistant," he said. "I'm Robert. I'm the program manager, and we're having one crisis after another this morning. We've got a ton of work waiting for you."

Tamera had to run to keep up with him as he took her up a flight of concrete stairs.

"Sabrina hasn't shown up, and Jeffrey has laryngitis," he called over his shoulder as he took the stairs two at a time.

Tamera had no idea who Sabrina or Jeffrey were, but she picked up Robert's urgency. Great, she thought. I might get to do something spectacular on my first day and show them all how talented I am.

"Okay, you can start in here," Robert said. He

pushed open a door, and Tamera found herself in a studio—mikes, tape decks, and all.

"Oh wow," she gasped. Even in her wildest dreams she hadn't imagined that she'd be a real DJ on her first day.

"Jeffrey gets in at eleven, and he hates mess," Robert said. "Get this place cleaned up, okay? There's a sink in the ladies' bathroom where you can wash up."

The door swung shut behind her, and Tamera found herself looking at the most disgusting pile of dirty dishes and cups she had ever seen. The coffee cups had lipstick around the edges, and someone had stubbed out cigarettes in the coffee spilled in the saucers. The plates had the remains of pizza stuck to them. The floor was full of more cigarette butts.

"Yuck!" Tamera said. This wasn't how she had imagined it at all.

She piled the dirty things onto a tray and carried them down to the ladies' bathroom. It wasn't easy to get them clean, and Tamera was splashed with soapy water and smeared with grease by the time she had finished. She was just carrying the dishes and cups back when she saw what looked like a homeless person slinking down the hall. He was unshaven, and his hair looked as if it hadn't been combed in a week. His dirty T-shirt stretched across a fat belly, and under it were torn, dirty jeans.

Tamera looked around, but there was nobody in sight. It was up to her to save the station in case he had come to rob them or was a crank with a grudge.

"Excuse me," she said politely as the man headed

for the nearest studio, "but you can't go in there. This is private property."

The man looked at her as if she was a worm. "What are you talking about, honey?" he growled. "I work here." He looked up as Robert came running down the hall.

"Robert, what's this creepy kid doing here?" he snapped. "She's bugging me."

"She's the new assistant, Tamera Campbell," Robert said.

"Well, tell her to keep out of my hair," the man said, giving Tamera a hard, unfriendly stare. He staggered into the studio, and the door swung shut behind him.

Robert gave Tamera an understanding smile. "Sorry, but he's not at his best in the morning," he said.

"Who is he?" Tamera asked.

"That's Beastman," Robert said. "Surely you've heard of him."

"That's Beastman?" Tamera's heart sank. He had sounded so young and hip on the air. There was no way she could ever ask him for an autograph. She wouldn't even want to.

"Did you get studio one finished yet?" Robert asked her.

"I still have to sweep the floor. You didn't tell me where the brooms were," Tamera said.

"In the closet at the end of the hall," Robert said, "and hurry. Jeffrey is a total neatness freak. He has hysterics if the studio isn't spotless when he comes for his shift at eleven, and the evening DJs always leave it like a pigsty."

Tamera raced to sweep up all the litter on the studio floor. She had just finished when an elegantly dressed man came in. He had a muffler wrapped around his mouth and throat. "Oh no, it still smells of smoke," he gasped. "I told them I had laryngitis, but I guess nobody cares if the listeners can hear me or not. Didn't anyone think of using the air freshener?" He pointed at Tamera. "Go get it at once. I can't work in here with this tobacco stink."

By the end of the morning Tamera was exhausted. Nobody had treated her like a person at all. They had seen her as a robot, only fit to do their grossest work for them.

She was just hoping to find out if there was a cafeteria and get some lunch when Robert called her again.

"Sabrina wants you in her office," he said.

"Sabrina?"

"You know her as Leopard Lady, I expect," Robert said. "Hurry, because she's not in a very good mood."

"Nobody is around here," Tamera muttered to herself. She told herself Sabrina would be different. Tamera would be extra nice and helpful and win Sabrina over with her personality. She tapped on the door and went in cautiously. "You needed help with something?" she asked.

A gorgeous, slim woman was sitting at a desk, examining her long, red fingernails.

"Oh, hi there, sweetie. You must be the new

gofer," she said, giving Tamera a smile. "I need a big favor. *Ebony* magazine is coming in for a photo op this afternoon, and I didn't get a chance to pick up the outfit I wanted to wear from the cleaners. Pop out and get it for me, would you?"

"Sure. No problem," Tamera said, glad to be given such an easy task and to get on Sabrina's good side at the same time.

She took the cleaner's receipt and ran down the stairs. It was only when she was outside the door that she looked at the receipt carefully. The cleaners was way across town!

It took her almost two hours and several changes of buses to get there and back again. When she came up the stairs she was met by a hysterical Sabrina.

"Where on earth have you been?" she demanded. "The photographer from *Ebony* was already here! My picture is going to be on the cover in this old thing!"

"I-I'm sorry," Tamera stammered. "I went as fast as I could, honesty."

"What did you do—walk? Crawl?"

"No, I went by bus," Tamera said, "but I had to change so many times and I missed a couple of connections."

"Bus?" Sabrina asked as if this was a dirty word. "Are you trying to tell you don't have a car?"

"I'm too young to drive yet," Tamera said.

"Of all the stupid things," Sabrina snapped. "What is wrong with Malcolm, hiring an assistant who can't even drive? What use will she be to anybody?"

"I'm really sorry," Tamera said again. "If I'd

known how long it would take, I would have said something and you could have found someone with a car to do it for you."

"Honey, you are totally clueless," Sabrina said. "If you didn't have a car, you should have taken a taxi. You'd better get your act together, sweetie, or you're out of here."

"So how was your day?" Ray greeted her as she arrived home. Tamera looked up to see Tia and Lisa looking at her expectantly. She swallowed hard. "Fine," she said with a bright smile. "Real busy but fun, you know."

"So what did you get to do?" Tia asked.

"All kinds of stuff," Tamera said. "I got to help Leopard Lady with her outfit for a photo shoot." She thought it wise not to add that she had personally blown the photo shoot for Leopard Lady, who now hated her guts.

"Cool!" Tia said.

"So how was *your* first day?" Tamera asked Tia, before she had to keep up her perkiness any longer.

"It was fine, too," Tia said. "They kept me really busy."

Tamera noted that Tia hadn't said her first day was great or wonderful, only fine. Maybe it hadn't been any better than her own first-day disaster. She'd have to get the truth out of Tia when they were alone.

It wasn't until they were up in their room, getting ready for bed, that Tamera finally had a chance to talk to her sister.

"Okay," she said. "Now, how was it really?"

"What are you talking about?" Tia asked.

"Your first day at work. How was it really?"

"It was fine, like I said."

"Tia, if it had really been great, you would have said great. If you said fine, then it must have stunk."

"You said yours was fine, too," Tia pointed out.

"Okay, well, mine wasn't so hot either," Tamera said.

"It wasn't?"

Tamera shook her head. "They were all so mean to me, Tia. Everybody was in a rush all the time, and they just yelled at me to do things. Sabrina—that's Leopard Lady's real name—got mad at me because she sent me clear across town to pick up her dry cleaning and it took me two hours. She expected me to take a taxi."

"You don't have money for taxis!"

"Right!" Tamera said. "And I had to wash disgusting coffee cups with lipstick on them. I'd have had less washing up to do at Rocket Burger, Tia."

"I had to do a lot of washing up, too," Tia said.

"You mean like lab equipment?"

"No—mainly their coffee cups, too."

Tamera laughed. "I guess this is what they mean by starting at the bottom, Tia. One day we'll be able to look back on this, when someone else is washing up *our* dirty cups."

"But we'll be nice to the kids who are doing the washing up, right?"

"They weren't nice to you at the lab?"

"Oh, they weren't mean like your Leopard Lady," Tia said, "but they take everything so seriously. And then there were the mice. . . ."

"Mice? You're working in a building infested with mice?"

"In cages," Tia said. "They breed them there, Tamera, to use in their experiments."

"Gross!"

"I know," Tia said. "And I'm supposed to clean out their cages. They're so sweet, Tamera. They stand up on their hind paws and wiffle their little noses at me and I feel so bad, knowing what they're going to be used for."

"What *are* they going to be used for?"

"They alter their genes to see if they still get diseases. Then they cut them open and examine their organs."

"Tia, that is so cruel."

"I know," Tia said. "Nobody else seems to care about it. I'm going to ask to be given another job. I couldn't face those sweet little faces every day."

"So how did Heather like it?"

"She just loved it. She's been asking intelligent questions all day. They let her take down data for them."

"Maybe they'll give you more interesting things to do when they see how smart you are."

"I hope so," Tia said. "It's hard to judge anything by the first day, isn't it?"

"I hope so," Tamera echoed. "Because if today was normal we're both in for a long summer."

Chapter 6

✪

When Tia went to bed that night, she couldn't stop thinking about the mice. Every time she closed her eyes she saw those hopeful little faces. She remembered how soft and warm they had felt against her hands.

Maybe I'll get used to it, she told herself. Maybe everyone feels like this at first. But then she decided that she didn't want to get used to it. She wouldn't ever think it was right. But now she was stuck with looking after the mice for the whole summer. She would feed them and keep them healthy so that they could be made sick and killed whenever the scientists needed them. And she knew that she couldn't do that. She would have to quit.

She went to work the next morning having made up her mind that it would be her last day on the job. She didn't say anything to Heather. It would be no use talking to her. Heather thought it was fine to kill helpless mice if it was to help science.

As Tia fed the mice for the last time, she looked at the little faces and her heart felt as if it was about to break.

"I'm sorry I have to leave you," she said. "But I can't do this."

Then a terrible, wonderful idea came into her head. She would set the mice free before she went. Mice were smart—they'd find ways to escape and hide. At least some of them would get away! She waited until Heather had left the room, and then she began emptying the cages. Soon the whole floor was covered with squeaking, scurrying mice.

At that moment Heather came back into the lab. "What are you doing?" she screamed as mice scurried in all directions.

"Setting them free," Tia said. "I think what they're doing here is cruel and wrong."

"Have you freaked out? You'll lose your job! Help me put them back quickly!"

"No way," Tia said. "And I don't want to go on working in a place like this!"

"But my father got you this job," Heather said angrily. "And you've probably wrecked some important experiments."

There was a yell from the doorway. Dr. Hauser, the lab director, was standing there, staring in horror. "What's going on here?" he demanded.

"She let out the mice," Heather said quickly. "I'll help you catch them again, Dr. Hauser."

"Get out of here. You're fired," Dr. Hauser yelled, pointing at Tia.

"You can't fire me. I quit," Tia said. She stepped carefully around the mice and walked past Dr. Hauser, who was already on his knees, trying to grab a mouse as it darted under a table.

Once she was outside the building a big smile spread across her face. She had actually done it. It felt so good.

But then it suddenly hit her—she had lost her job. She had no work and nothing to do for the summer, and she had probably lost a friend, too. And what was she going to tell them at home? Tamera would understand, she was sure, but her mother and Ray had been so proud of her for getting the job in the lab. Tia decided not to say anything until she had another job lined up.

As she walked toward the bus stop, she tried to think. She definitely needed to earn money, and there was no way she was going back to Rocket Burger. She remembered Denise saying that they could probably use more counselors at the nature camp.

Maybe I could do that, she thought. It might be fun, and I might learn a lot about nature, too.

She made up her mind to call Denise that afternoon. But she wouldn't say anything to anyone at home until she was sure that nature camp was something she really wanted to do.

Meanwhile Tamera had decided that every day at Happenin' Radio was equally crazy. People were always running around and yelling. It didn't seem to matter how hard she worked—someone was always waiting for her to do something else.

At least I won't gain weight this summer, she thought. I haven't had a chance to eat in two days.

She was hopeful she'd have time to buy herself a sandwich when she was sent out with the lunch orders. A sandwich truck pulled up outside the station, and Robert sent Tamera down with a whole list of orders. "Okay, Sabrina wants turkey breast on whole wheat, no mayo and no pickle and sparkling water to go with it, and Jeffrey wants corned beef on rye with mustard, not mayo, and apple juice and . . ." Tamera tried to keep them all straight. But as she headed for the stairs, the door to the technicians' room opened.

"Are you going to get lunches?" one of the techs asked her. Then before she could answer he went on. "Great. Bring me Swiss cheese and tomato on a French roll. And Doug will have a chili dog. . . ." By the time she got to the stairs, Tamera's head was buzzing.

Why didn't I write this all down? she asked herself. Then she gave herself the answer—because nobody gave me time.

She filled the orders as she hoped she remembered them and delivered twelve lunches to what she hoped were the right people. It only took a couple of seconds for her to realize that she had blown it.

"Wait—this has mayo on it! I ordered it on wheat,

not white! There's pickle on this! I said no pickle! Can't you get anything right?"

Everyone was yelling at her at once. Suddenly something inside Tamera snapped. "Okay. That's it," she yelled back. "I'm not a robot, you know. Go get your own lunches next time."

There was a sudden silence. Tamera looked around. None of the faces looking at her was friendly. "I was trying my hardest," she said, "but whatever I do, it's not good enough for you guys. Find someone else to yell at. I quit!" Then she stalked out.

After she had cooled down, she realized what she had done. She had given up her dream job. Now she realized that it wasn't a dream job after all. A dream job was where everybody got along and had fun, not where everybody was constantly stressed out. But now what was she going to do with her whole summer?

Tamera walked aimlessly through the streets, trying to get her head in order. Everyone had been so excited and proud of her for getting such a glamorous job. Now she'd have to tell them that she didn't have it anymore. But she knew she couldn't have taken another day like that. She wished Tia wasn't at work. She badly needed someone to talk to right now.

Down the street an old school bus pulled up, and a group of teenagers got out.

"Hey, Tamera!" a voice called. Denise was waving at her.

"What are you doing here?" she asked as Tamera came up to her. "Out for a lunchtime stroll?"

"Something like that," Tamera said. "What are *you* doing here? I thought you were out at some nature camp."

"I am," Denise said. She turned to her friends. "I'll catch up with you guys at the coffee shop. Save me a place."

"We only had a half day of training today," Denise said, coming over to Tamera. "It's training all this week, and then we meet the campers next Monday."

"So how's it going so far?" Tia asked.

"It's a blast. We're having so much fun. We have to do all the stuff we're going to be teaching the kids, so we're working with clay and finger paints and leaf prints and learning how to roll canoes. I just love it. How is your job going? I guess it's kind of different in the real world, huh?"

"Very different," Tamera said. "A lot of pressure."

"But worth it, working with all those stars," Denise said.

Tamera swallowed hard.

"It's too bad I couldn't get you and Tia to join me at camp," Denise went on. "We're still a couple of counselors short. That means a whole lot of kids who signed up won't be able to come. We have to have one counselor for every five kids."

Thoughts were rushing around inside Tamera's head. Part of her didn't want Denise to know that she had quit her dream job. But another voice inside her head was screaming that she should take this chance, because she might not get another.

"That's too bad," she said to Denise. "I mean, all those poor little kids who can't go to camp."

Denise shrugged. "What can you do?"

"Maybe I could switch jobs," Tamera said.

Denise's eyes opened wide. "Give up your dream job?"

Tamera decided to come clean. "It wasn't such a dream job, Denise," she said. "They weren't nice people, and that place was a madhouse. Everyone was stressed out all the time, and all they did was yell. All I got to do was wash up yucky coffee cups with lipstick on them."

"So are you saying you don't want to go on working there?" Denise asked.

"I'm saying that I just quit," Tamera said.

"Are you serious?" Denise asked. "You were so excited about it. What happened to writing the scripts and working with Beastman and Leopard Lady?"

"Beastman turned out to be a real beast," Tamera said. "And Leopard Lady was worse. I've learned one thing, Denise. Just because a job is in a glamorous place doesn't mean it's a fun job. Maybe I'd have more fun with your kids at the camp."

"Tamera, that's great news," Denise said. "Why don't you come and meet my friends and the camp director? Then you could see if you want to join us."

"Okay," Tamera said. "It's either that or Roger with his lawn mower. What have I got to lose?"

"Great. Come on then," Denise said. "The others are waiting at the coffee shop."

Tamera imagined going home and telling Tia that she was no longer a high-powered production assistant at Happenin' Radio. She was only a camp counselor instead. And how could she ever tell her dad after she had bugged him to get her the job? He would think she couldn't handle hard work. He probably wouldn't even understand what it was like, and he'd be disappointed in her. And Lisa would be disappointed that she'd never get to wear the outfit she was making.

Maybe she'd just forget to mention at home that she had switched jobs, at least until she saw that she could handle being a counselor.

"Just one thing, Denise," Tamera said. "Don't mention this to my family if you meet them. I'll tell them when I'm good and ready."

Chapter 7

The next morning Tia got up very early and showered and dressed before Tamera woke up. She wanted to be ready for her first day at camp before Tamera woke up. She had managed to talk to Denise the night before, and Denise had seemed happy she was going to help out. At least I'll be somewhere where I'm wanted, Tia thought. She shoved a swimsuit and towel into her backpack. When she came back from brushing her teeth in the bathroom she stopped in surprise.

"Hey, Tamera, how come you're dressed like that today?" she asked, looking at Tamera's green T-shirt and khaki shorts. "Do they let you wear shorts to work?"

"Oh, this?" Tamera seemed flustered. "It's—ecology day at the station. We all get to dress like we're saving the environment."

"Cool," Tia said. She noticed Tamera looking at her strangely.

"How come you're wearing shorts?" Tamera asked.

"It doesn't matter what I wear under my lab coat," Tia said. "I thought this would be a good way to keep cool. It gets hot in that lab."

Then she hurried out of the room before Tamera could ask her any more embarrassing questions.

Tia grabbed a quick toasted bagel for breakfast and hastily packed a lunch. All she wanted to do was get out of the house in a hurry.

She tiptoed to the front door and slipped out without saying good-bye to anyone. She was halfway down the front path when the front door opened behind her and Tamera slipped out. Tamera did a double take when she saw Tia.

"Tia—I didn't hear you go out," she said. "I thought you were still upstairs."

"You're going to work earlier today?" Tia asked.

"Uh-uh. I thought I'd get a jump on cleaning up the place," Tamera said. "How about you?"

"I thought I'd clean up the place, too," Tia said.

They walked to the bus stop together. A number fifteen bus pulled up. Tamera didn't move.

"Tamera, isn't that your bus?" Tia asked, giving her sister a shove.

'Oh—uh—right. Whoops. Too late. I'll get the next one. They come along all the time. And I am kind of early. I'll wait and see you on your bus first." She nudged Tia. "You're in luck. You take the fifty-eight, don't you?"

"Usually, but I think the forty-four is just as easy for me."

"How come? That doesn't go right past the university, does it?"

"No, but . . . I like the forty-four. It goes through the park."

"Oh, the park. That's nice," Tamera said. "Maybe I'll take the forty-four with you and keep you company."

"You don't have to do that," Tia said hurriedly.

"But I'd like to," Tamera said.

The bus arrived and the girls got on.

"This is your stop coming up, right?" Tia asked.

"I could go a little farther," Tamera said.

Tia shook her head. "After this the bus swings to the left. You'd have to walk for miles back to the radio station. Go on, quick. Ring the bell."

Tamera knocked Tia's hand so that it missed the bell. "Whoops, too late," she said. "I guess I'll have to ride to the next stop now."

"What is with you today?" Tia demanded. "You sure are acting weird."

"It's just the stress of a high-powered job," Tamera said. "My mind is on other things."

The bus slowed for the next stop. Tia almost pushed Tamera off the bus. "You haven't forgotten where you work, have you?" she called after Tamera as the doors closed.

She heaved a sigh of relief. She thought she'd never get rid of Tamera. If Tamera had stayed on the bus Tia would have had to have ridden it all the way to the university and then sprint back to the summer camp meeting point.

She got off at the next stop and headed to the square where she was to meet the counselors. As she turned the corner she did a double take—Tamera was turning into the street from the opposite direction. Tamera saw her at about the same moment and looked alarmed.

"What are you doing here?" Tia called.

"What are *you* doing here?" Tamera countered.

"I'm . . . swinging by the doughnut shop," Tia said quickly. "They make great doughnuts at the little coffee shop on the square."

"That's where I'm going, too," Tamera said.

They turned into the square together. A yellow school bus was parked outside the doughnut shop. Several young people in outdoorsy clothes were standing by the bus.

Tia wasn't sure what to do next. She just prayed that Tamera would buy a doughnut and then go quickly.

Before they could go into the shop, Denise stepped out from behind the school bus.

"Yo, Tia, Tamera, over here," she called. "Come and meet the camp director. I've told him all about you."

Tia looked at Tamera. Tamera looked at Tia.

"You're going to be working at the camp?" Tia asked.

Tamera nodded. "You, too?"

Tia nodded as well. "What happened to your job?"

she asked. "I thought it was your dream job. Did you get fired?"

"No, I quit," Tamera said. "I couldn't take it, Tia. It was the most stressful place I've ever seen. All they did was yell. I really worked my hardest, but it was never good enough. So I quit. What about you? I thought you'd found your dream job, too."

"I thought so too, until I saw the mice," Tia said. "I couldn't do it, Tamera. Every time I closed my eyes, I saw their little faces. How could I feed them and take care of them all summer, knowing they were going to be killed? It wasn't right."

"So you quit?"

A big smile spread across Tia's face. "I was going to, only they fired me first."

"Tia, the perfect scientist, got fired? What for?"

"Letting all the mice out of their cages might have had something to do with it," Tia said.

Tamera's face lit up. "Tia, you didn't."

"I did so. It felt great, Tamera. You should have seen the lab director down on his knees, trying to catch them again. They were running all over the floor and up the walls. I figured at least some of them had the chance to escape."

"Tia, I'd never have believed it of you," Tamera said. "Good for you. I think it's great. But how come you didn't tell me about it sooner?"

Tia looked down at her sneakers. "I wanted to make sure I could handle this job first," she said. "I haven't told my mom yet either. I don't really know what to say to her. She was so proud of me for having a real job at the university."

"I know how you feel," Tamera said. "I've been worrying about what to tell my dad. He got me the job at the radio station. I kind of feel like I let him down."

"I'm sure he'll understand, Tamera," Tia said. "He wouldn't want you to be unhappy all summer."

"I guess not," Tamera said uncertainly. "I suppose we do have to tell my dad and your mom?"

"Of course we have to tell them, Tamera. We can't go on pretending all summer!"

"Okay. If everything goes well today and they don't fire us and we decide we can handle the outdoors, then let's tell them together at dinner tonight. There's safety in numbers."

Tia smiled. "Great idea," she said.

"I hope this job turns out to be fun, Tia. I mean, nobody could know less about the great outdoors than me."

"Except maybe me," Tia said. "But now we're doing it together, I don't care, Tamera. We'll fake it together, right?"

"Right," Tamera said, with a big smile.

They followed Denise over to a tall, skinny college-age guy.

"This is my cousin, Scott Draper," she said. "He's running the camp. I told him all about you."

Scott looked like the complete outdoor type, lean and tanned, wearing huge hiking boots and well-worn khaki shorts.

"Hi, girls. I'm glad you could help us out," he said. "I hated to say no to those little kids, but we have a rule about one counselor for every five campers. Now we can invite ten more campers. Climb on board the bus. We're ready to go. We'll save the introductions for circle time at the site."

The bus was almost full of kids their age and older as Tia and Tamera climbed on board. They smiled and said hi as they made their way to an empty seat. Then the diesel engine roared to life and conversation was impossible after that. Tia was glad that the noise was too loud for conversation. She was feeling very nervous about her first day at camp. She liked to do things well, and she wasn't at all sure that a nature camp was something she was going to be good at.

At last the city turned into suburbs, and then Tia caught a glimpse of Lake Erie sparkling in the distance. The bus drove in through a gateway with a metal sign over it that read Howard Morgan Nature Reserve. The moment the bus passed through the gate, it was like being in another world. Trees grew thickly along the bumpy trail. A flight of geese passed over, calling to each other as they flew. A rabbit scampered alongside the road. At last the bus pulled up in a clearing beside the lake. In front of them was a grassy area leading down to a sandy beach with a lifeguard chair in the middle. Brightly painted canoes were chained together at the water's edge. There were picnic tables under the trees and two log cabins that were rest rooms.

Tia glanced at Tamera. "Pretty, huh?"

"Pretty primitive," Tamera whispered. "There's a lot of trees between us and civilization. Are there bears here, do you think? Or how about wolves? Or snakes?"

"Shut up," Tia said, glancing around nervously. "It's only ten miles from the city, Tamera. We'll be fine."

"I hope so," Tamera said.

Denise came up to them. "Come on, I'll show you where we meet for circle time. It's over here, through the trees."

Tia and Tamera followed her to an area under the trees where logs had been arranged in a circle.

"There are ants on this log," Tamera whispered to Tia. "You don't think they're the type of ants that eat people alive, do you? I saw it once on *National Geographic*. They ate this big zebra until there was just bones left."

"Tamera, will you shut up," Tia said, hastily brushing the ants off the log. "Those ants are in Africa."

"They could have migrated. Lots of things do," Tamera said. "They could have come here with some bananas or something and nobody noticed until now. I just don't want to look down and find my leg being eaten alive."

"Euwww," Tia said. "Tamera, stop grossing me out." She had enough worries without Tamera finding new ones for her.

"Okay, everyone. Good morning and welcome," Scott said. "We have two new counselors to introduce today. I want you all to welcome Tia and Tamera. You have to sort out which is which." He gave a nervous chuckle.

"I'm the pretty one," Tamera said quickly.

"And I'm the smart one," Tia added, not wanting to be outdone.

The other counselors laughed.

"Hi, I'm Brandon," the boy sitting next to Tia said. They went around the circle saying names. Tia tried to remember all the names, but there were at least twenty counselors and she got lost about halfway around. At least they all seemed friendly, except for one girl. She was gorgeous and acted as if she knew it. Her pale yellow tank top showed off her light brown skin. Her hair was braided back from her face into a ponytail of hundreds of little braids.

Tamera nudged Tia. "I bet she can't light fires and cross rope bridges and skin rabbits," she whispered to Tia.

"She'd worry she'd break a fingernail," Tia whispered back. They grinned at each other.

The girl was sitting next to Scott and was looking at Tia and Tamera as if they were two worms that had just crawled out from under a log.

"And this is Roxanne," Scott said. "She's my assistant director this year. She knows everything you need to know about the great outdoors."

"Including which is the quickest way back to the city," Tia whispered. She got the impression that Roxanne heard her because she gave Tia a long, hard stare.

"Maybe you'd like to tell us just a little about your-selves," Scott said, looking at Tia and Tamera. "Have you worked at a camp like this before?"

"Not exactly like this," Tia said. "But I did work at a day camp last summer for a while. It included activities like hiking."

"And I helped her out once and took her kids on a nature hike," Tamera added. She didn't add that she had gotten the kids lost and had gotten Tia fired.

"Great," Scott said. "So you probably know the outdoor code pretty well then."

The outdoor code? Tia began to panic. Was that something you learned, like the pledge of allegiance?

"Let's just run through it quickly," Scott said. "You start, Roxanne."

"Let's see," Roxanne said in a bored voice. "Always leave an area as you found it. Take out everything you brought in. Only hike on marked trails and—"

"Fine, Roxanne," Scott cut in before she could go on. "How about someone else. Brandon?"

"Don't light fires without permission and only in designated fire pits."

"Josh?"

"Always swim or hike with a buddy," the next boy said.

"Denise?"

"Tell someone where you are going."

They all know it, Tia thought, giving Tamera a worried glance. She was hoping Scott wouldn't call on her because she couldn't think of anything to say.

"Tamera? How about you?" Scott asked.

"Stay away from snakes and bears?" Tamera suggested. Everyone laughed. Tia was glad she hadn't said something dumb like that.

"Good advice," Scott said. "But I hope you don't meet too many of either." He picked up his clipboard. "Let me just remind you that we have training for the rest of the week. On Monday morning the kids get here, and then the fun really starts. Before then you have a lot to learn about surviving in the wilderness."

Tia and Tamera glanced nervously at each other.

Scott glanced at his board again. "What we'll be doing this morning is familiarizing ourselves with the animals and bugs the kids will find here. I'm going to set up charts and displays to help you identify the various birds, mammals, reptiles, and insects. I want you to study them well, then we'll go into the field and try to find some of them. I'm sure most of you know all this already." He looked at Tia and Tamera.

"Oh, right," Tamera said. She leaned across to Tia. "I know a bird from a mammal," she muttered under her breath, "and I'm not even sure about that when it comes to bats."

Tia headed straight for the first chart. She got a notebook out of her backpack and started making notes. Tamera stared at a poster showing at least a hundred birds. They all looked almost the same to her. "I think I'll become the reptile expert," she said to Tia. "There aren't so many of them."

She walked across the clearing to where a display

of reptiles was set up. There was a real frog in a glass cage, some newts and a turtle swimming around, plus a snake skin and pictures of snakes and lizards. Tamera made sure she learned what the poisonous ones looked like.

She looked up from studying reptiles when she heard sounds of activity coming from the beach. Tamera saw Scott down there, unchaining the canoes with another guy who hadn't been in the circle. Her eyes opened wider. The guys at the circle had been okay but a little nerdy. This guy was definitely a hunk. His white lifeguard tank top contrasted with his copper-colored skin and showed off his swimmer's body.

Denise came up to Tamera. "How are you doing?" she asked.

"Doing some serious studying," Tamera said.

"Great," Denise said. "What have you learned?"

"That I've discovered a rare animal," Tamera said.

"You have? Where?"

Tamera pointed down at the lake. "How about a genuine hunk?" she asked. "Who is he, Denise? He is so cute."

"That's Patrick, one of the camp lifeguards," Denise said. "You're right, he is cute. See, I promised you cute guys, didn't I?"

"I think I might just have to specialize in water beetles," Tamera said. "That will give me an excuse to be by the lake all the time."

Denise laughed. "You're terrible, Tamera," she said.

Then Denise wandered over to the next study area, leaving Tamera still watching Patrick. She noticed how easily he picked up the canoes and how his dark eyes lit up when he laughed at something Scott said to him. Now all she had to do was find a way to meet him!

Chapter 8

⊚

*A*n hour later Scott called all the counselors together again. Tamera just prayed there wouldn't be a test on what they were supposed to have learned. Patrick was still down by the lake. Obviously he didn't have to learn about bugs and frogs.

"Okay, let's put what we've learned into practice," Scott said. "Let's look around the camp area and see how many living creatures we can find and identify."

Tamera moved close to Tia. Almost immediately someone spotted a butterfly.

"What are we looking at here?" Scott asked.

"A swallowtail," Tia said before anyone else.

Down by a little creek they found a frog. Tia knew its correct name, too. Everyone was looking at her in admiration. Tamera was impressed. Tia had to be the world's fastest learner.

As they went on, Tia knew everything.

"I'm really glad you joined us, Tia," Tamera heard Scott say. "You'll be a real asset to our camp."

Tamera tried not to feel annoyed. She just hoped this wasn't going to turn into another of those situations in which Tia did everything better than her. Fine, let her be queen of the outdoors, Tamera told herself. I'm going to meet Patrick first.

She slipped away from the rest of the group and wandered through the trees to the lakefront. Patrick was wiping down canoes.

"Hi," Tamera said.

Patrick looked up and smiled. He had such a wonderful smile that her heart did a flip-flop.

"I was wondering," she began, not sure what to say next, "if you knew where there's a drinking fountain," she finished, babbling the first thing that came into her head.

Patrick grinned. "A drinking fountain? We're in the wilderness here," he said. "There's no drinking fountain."

"Oh no." Tamera sighed. "I'm going to be really thirsty by the time we go home."

Patrick looked surprised. "Didn't you bring a drink with your lunch?"

"Lunch? We were supposed to bring lunch?" she asked.

"You didn't think there'd be a McDonald's out here, did you?" he asked, looking amused at her discomfort.

"No! Of course not!" Tamera said defensively. "It's

just that this is my first day and I knew they finished by lunchtime yesterday, so I didn't think I'd need a lunch."

"You'll need a lunch," Patrick said. "Scott believes in working people hard."

"I'm going to die of starvation," Tamera said.

Patrick looked at Tamera's panicked face. "Tell you what," he said. "I'll share mine with you if you like. My mom made me two huge tuna fish sandwiches today. I'll probably only want one of them. You can have the other."

"I can?" Tamera beamed. "That is so nice of you. Tuna sandwiches are my favorite, and I'm the only person in my house who likes them, so we never get them."

"Sure. No problem," Patrick said. "And I think Scott always brings an extra bottle of water. I'd share mine, but I always need it all. It gets hot here by the lake."

"It's okay," Tamera said. "Thanks a million. I owe you one. I'll have to bake you brownies sometime. I bake a mean brownie."

"Sounds good," Patrick said, smiling at her.

Tamera wanted to stay longer, but she saw the rest of the group moving off through the trees.

"I have to be getting back or they'll have found a lesser spotted nuthatch without me," she said. She gave Patrick a winning smile as she ran to catch up with them.

"I've just met the cutest boy," she whispered to Tia.

"Where?" Tia said, looking around.

"Down by the lake. Oh no," she added. "I didn't even tell him my name!"

"You'll have plenty of time to tell him your name, Tamera," Tia said. 'We're stuck here all summer, remember?"

Just then Scott's whistle called them all together and he had them split up and see how many creatures they could find in ten minutes.

Tia headed down toward the lake. She was sure it was much easier to see a lot of different forms of wildlife where the water met the land. She was standing on the shore when a guy she didn't know came running up to her.

'Here," he said, thrusting a sandwich into her hands.

"What's this for?" Tia wondered if it was part of a camp joke.

"It's the tuna sandwich," the guy said.

"A tuna sandwich?" Tia said, looking at the guy suspiciously. "Why are you giving me a tuna sandwich?"

"Because you wanted it." The guy was looking puzzled, too.

"But I hate tuna," Tia said.

Now the guy was looking even more puzzled. "You hate tuna? But I thought . . ." He shook his head. "Okay, forget it then." He took the sandwich back and strode away down the beach.

Tamera came up to Tia.

"Tamera, I have just met a really weird guy," Tia

said. "He was acting very strange. Do you think that maybe there are crazy people down by the lake?"

"I don't know," Tamera said. "I just know that I met a gorgeous guy who was totally sweet and not at all crazy."

"Lucky for you," Tia said. "This one was cute, but I hope he's not part of the camp staff."

Suddenly Tamera grabbed Tia's arm. "Look over there. That's my cute lifeguard. Isn't he gorgeous?"

"Wait," Tia said. "My crazy guy is coming toward us. Let's get out of here before he gives me more tuna sandwiches."

A light went on in Tamera's head. "That's the crazy guy coming up the path now?"

"Yeah. Let's get out of here," Tia said.

"And he tried to give you a tuna sandwich?"

"Yeah. Can you believe it? I'm just standing there, minding my own business, and he puts this tuna sandwich in my hands and tells me I like tuna. Totally weird, huh?"

Tamera was grinning. "Tia, he thought you were me," she said. "He promised to share his lunch with me."

"Oh no," Tia said. "He must think that I'm a total nut case."

Patrick came out of the trees and stopped in front of the twins. He looked confused and then shocked.

"There are two of you," he said at last.

"Right," Tia and Tamera said together.

"And I promised a tuna sandwich to one of you?"

"Me," Tamera said.

73

"And I gave it to the other one, right?"

"Right," Tia said.

An embarrassed grin spread across his face. "Boy, do I feel like a fool," he said. He turned to Tia. "No wonder you looked at me as if I was a dangerous maniac." He started to laugh. Tia laughed, too. Patrick's eyes were smiling into hers. She felt her heart beating faster.

"You want to join me for lunch, if I promise not to give you any more tuna sandwiches?" he asked Tia.

"Sure, I'd love to."

"Yeah, we'd love to," Tamera echoed quickly, just in case the invitation had been for Tia only.

"I'll meet you at the picnic tables," Patrick said. "Save me a place."

The moment he was out of earshot Tamera grabbed Tia's arm. "Let's get one thing straight," she said. "I saw him first. He was my cute guy and your crazy guy, remember?"

"Hey, calm down, Tamera," Tia said. "He only wants to have lunch with me."

"Lunch with *us*," Tamera corrected. "He wanted to have lunch with us."

"Okay. Whatever," Tia said with a shrug. "Stop making a big thing of this, Tamera. He's just a friendly guy being friendly."

"He was smiling at you," Tamera said.

"Really?" Tia tried not to sound too interested.

"So I wanted to warn you to butt out right now. If either of us gets him, it makes sense that it's me, because he and I have a lot in common."

"Like what?"

"We both like tuna sandwiches. You hate tuna. That means he'd make a better boyfriend for me than for you."

"Tamera, I don't think many relationships are made because of tuna sandwiches," Tia said.

"Hah! So you do like him," Tamera said. "I knew it. I saw that secret little smile you tried to give him."

"What smile? I was just being friendly," Tia said. "I'm not interested, okay? I'm too mature to go chasing after every cute guy I meet. I need someone who is my intellectual equal, as well as cute."

"Tia, guys at your intellectual level are dorks or robots," Tamera said.

"And guys with your intellectual level are just graduating from kindergarten," Tia said.

The two sisters stood there, glaring at each other. Tia laughed uneasily. "Come on, Tamera. We've just met the guy. We know nothing about him. I'm sure he already has a girlfriend and we're wasting our time fighting over him."

"I don't care if he already has a girlfriend," Tamera said. "You're forgetting my dynamic personality that no guy can resist. If I go after him, he's mine!"

Tia spluttered. "Yeah, right," she said.

Tamera gave Tia a long stare. "Just wait and see," she said.

As they headed for the picnic tables, Tia watched her sister hurrying eagerly ahead, already looking around for Patrick. Was it true that he had given her a secret smile, as Tamera said?

She went to pick up her backpack from where it was stacked and looked up to see Patrick standing beside her.

"I'm really sorry about the tuna sandwich," he said. "I want to curl up with embarrassment every time I think about it."

"Forget it," Tia said. "It was a very understandable mistake. People mix us up all the time."

"I don't even like tuna that much," Patrick whispered, bending his head close to Tia's.

"You don't?" She couldn't help smiling. Wait until Tamera heard this.

Patrick shook his head. "My mom loves it so I get tuna sandwiches every time she makes my lunch. Which should tell me that I'd better get up in time to make my own lunch in future, right?" he added.

That was just what Tia had been thinking. Could this guy read her thoughts?

"I wasn't going to say anything," Tia said, laughing.

"Tia! Patrick! Over here. I've saved you seats," Tamera was yelling.

Patrick gave Tia another little smile as they went to join Tamera. As she sat at the picnic table with Patrick beside her, she found herself wondering. She had told Tamera that she wasn't interested, but maybe she was. It was about time she had another boyfriend and a summer romance might be fun. But she'd have to fight Tamera for him, and that wouldn't be a good idea.

I'll just wait and see how it goes, Tia told herself.

I'll be friendly and if it goes on from there, fine. We'll just have to see which one of us he likes best.

After lunch they had a session on water safety. They went into the rest rooms to change into swimsuits. As Tia put on her dark green Speedo, she looked across and saw Tamera putting on her white lace bikini.

"And you thought I was the dumb sister," Tamera said, grinning. "I put this in my bag just in case any of the guys were cute."

"Tamera, that is totally unsuitable for camp," Tia said.

"But great for getting guys to notice me," Tamera said.

Tia watched out of the corner of her eye as she put her hair up into a ponytail. If only she'd known that Patrick was going to be here, then maybe she could have brought a bikini, too.

This is crazy, she told herself. I'm not competing with Tamera for a guy.

"I just hope that the fish don't nibble away at the shoestrings that hold that thing together," Tia said as she prepared to go to the lake.

"What fish?" Tamera asked, looking worried.

"This lake is full of huge fish," Tia said. "I saw them that time I went out on Paul's sailboat—whole schools of monster fish all swimming around down there."

"You're putting me on," Tamera said nervously. "I never heard of fish that eat bikini straps."

"They might think they're worms," Tia said.

"You're just jealous because you didn't think of wearing a bikini and Patrick's going to notice me," Tamera said.

"If Patrick likes me, it will be for myself and not for my itsy-bitsy bikini," Tia said smoothly.

The other counselors were waiting on the beach. Several of the guys whistled when they saw Tamera.

"I wouldn't dress like that when the campers get here," Roxanne said dryly. "You obviously don't know what ten-year-old boys are like. I found a frog in my makeup bag last year. Don't give them any chances to play jokes on you."

"That's right. Dress for survival," Denise added.

Scott called them all to the water's edge.

"First I want to make sure you know our lifeguards," he said. "Patrick is wearing the red shorts, and Roxanne is also a qualified lifeguard, and so is Brandon. They'll be taking over when Patrick is on a break."

Roxanne gave everyone an "I'm so wonderful" smile.

"I know we have trained lifeguards on duty at all times," Scott went on, "but I want every one of you to be prepared and know what to do in case of an emergency so we're going to run through all the rescue procedures."

Scott went through first aid drills with them and had Patrick demonstrate the rescue equipment.

"If Patrick needs a volunteer to demonstrate CPR, I'll race you for it," Tamera whispered to Tia. But

Scott had brought a CPR dummy for them to practice on.

Then they had to get in the water for water safety drills and to practice launching a canoe in a hurry. Tamera kept looking up to see what Patrick was doing, but Scott was keeping him very busy demonstrating things.

"I'm pooped," Tia whispered to Tamera.

"Me, too," Tamera said. "If this is tiring, just think what it will be like when the kids are here."

"Okay, everyone. Take a break," Scott called. "Free swim for half an hour."

Tia flopped into the lake and swam out with slow, easy strokes. She turned on her back and lay looking at the clear blue of the sky. She felt herself beginning to relax. This was going to be a fun job, she decided. Nice people, blue water, warm sun—a perfect way to spend the summer.

A scream behind her made her turn over in a hurry. She noticed how far from shore she had drifted. She just hoped that her stories about big fish weren't really true. She didn't like the thought of being out here with goodness-knows-what swimming below her. She looked around and there was Tamera, waving her arms desperately.

"What's up?" Tia yelled.

"A cramp. I've got a cramp in my foot," Tamera was yelling. "Help. I think I'm drowning."

"Hold on, I'm coming." Tia started to swim over to her.

"Not you, dummy," Tamera muttered under her

breath. She turned herself around until she was facing Patrick, sitting in the lifeguard's chair. "Help," she called, waving at him.

"Tamera! Even you couldn't stoop that low," Tia said.

"Chill out," Tamera said. She went on waving her arms. "Save me," she called.

"What's wrong?" Patrick called to her, not leaving his seat.

"I've got a cramp. Help," Tamera called. "My foot hurts me."

"Massage it," Patrick called back.

"But I can't move it," Tamera said dramatically.

"Swim with the other one," Patrick yelled back.

"What kind of lifeguard are you?" Tamera demanded. "Aren't you going to rescue me?"

A big grin spread across Patrick's face. "I figure that anyone who can carry on a conversation has enough strength to swim to shore. Besides, you can stand where you are."

"But I'm getting weaker," Tamera said. "I think I'm drowning. I can feel myself slipping away. Somebody save me."

There was a splash on the beach as someone dove in. A head broke the surface close to Tamera. It was a head covered in tiny braids.

"Just relax and let me tow you," Roxanne said. She wrapped her arm over Tamera and started dragging her toward the shore.

"Wait, you've got it wrong. I wasn't really drowning. It was a rescue drill," Tamera protested as Roxanne dragged her in. "Weren't we still practicing rescue drills? Let go of me. I can swim on my own. Help, you're choking me."

Tia followed behind, laughing so hard that she could hardly swim. That would teach Tamera not to be sneaky!

Chapter 9

⊚⊚

"Tamera, are you ready? We have to leave," Tia called through the bathroom door the next morning. "You've been in there for hours."

"Just coming," Tamera called. She opened the door and came out. She was wearing a Hawaiian print halter top and tiny white denim shorts. On her head was a white baseball cap decorated with sequins. Her ponytail poked through the back of it. It was a mass of little curls.

"Wow!" Tia exclaimed. "Are you going to camp or trying out for *Baywatch*?"

"Looking good, huh," Tamera said. "Today Patrick can't fail to notice me."

"You never give up, do you?" Tia said. "Tamera, if he was really interested in you, he'd have rescued you yesterday. Instead of that he just laughed."

"Yeah, I have to admit that was kind of mean of him."

"Well, it was very funny," Tia said. "You should have seen your face when Roxanne wanted to do CPR on you."

"That girl really bugged me," Tamera said. "I kept telling her that she was holding my head under the water, and she said it was standard procedure to stop the victim from struggling. I bet she did it on purpose."

"That will teach you not to fake drowning again," Tia said. "Patrick knew what you were trying to do. Girls probably pull that stunt around cute lifeguards all the time."

"He'll forget about yesterday when he's dazzled by my beauty today," Tamera said.

"Tamera, I think you live in a dream world sometimes," Tia said. "Guys like girls who are friendly and easy to talk to."

"Like you?"

"Maybe," Tia said.

"No way," Tamera said. "Guys like girls who look great. By the end of today, he'll be eating out of my hand."

"Why? Are you going to be carrying around another tuna sandwich with you?" Tia asked, laughing.

Tamera gave her a withering stare and swept down the stairs.

"Oh, and don't forget to bring a lunch today," Tia called.

She glanced at herself in the bedroom mirror. She did look kind of blah in her khaki shorts and white camp shirt. Could it be that Tamera was right and guys did go for girls who looked great? She was tempted to run and change, but she didn't want Tamera to think that she was going after Patrick.

Tia heard Ray yelling that he'd give them a ride if they hurried up. She ran downstairs after Tamera. Ray was standing in the driveway, beside the car. His eyes opened wide in surprise when he saw Tamera.

"Just what sort of camp is this, Tamera?" he demanded.

"Regular day camp," Tamera said. "Why?"

"And you think you're wearing a suitable outfit for a counselor?" Ray asked. "Don't you think you should look professional, like your sister?"

"Boring like my sister, you mean?" Tamera began, but Ray cut in.

"You've already messed up on one job this summer, Tamera. I want you to make a good impression in this one."

"Dad, we're still in training," Tamera said. "The kids don't get here until next Monday, so it doesn't really matter what we wear. Is it my fault that I want to look good?" She glanced across at Tia as she slid into the backseat of the car.

Tia didn't say anything as she climbed in beside her. Let Tamera make a fool of herself, she decided. Then he'll have to decide that he likes me.

"Today we learn to find our way through the forest," Scott said. "I expect all of you know how to use a compass."

"Yeah, I used one in geometry last year," Tamera said. "And a protractor."

"Not that sort of compass, Tamera," Tia said. "He means the kind of compass that points to magnetic north."

"Oh," Tamera said, looking annoyed that Tia had been able to show her smarts again.

"We'll be taking a long hike this morning, so bring your water bottles with you," Scott said. "I hope you've all followed my advice and brought plenty of water today. And I hope you're all wearing good strong boots."

"Sort of," Tamera muttered, looking down at her flimsy sandals.

"Are you coming with us, Patrick?" Roxanne asked.

"I might as well. I've got nobody to guard until the kids get here," Patrick said.

Tamera smiled and took off the big sweatshirt she had been wearing on the bus.

"Are you thinking of hiking in that?" Roxanne asked, looking amused as her eyes traveled over Tamera's halter top, teeny shorts, and flimsy sandals.

"Sure. Why not?" Tamera said.

"You're going to be sorry," Roxanne said.

"Don't worry about me. I'm used to hiking," Tamera said. "I was born and brought up in the great outdoors."

"She's just jealous because I look better than she does today," Tamera whispered to Tia as they followed Scott to the trailhead.

They set off into the forest. Patrick came to walk beside Tamera.

"Are you wearing sandals in case you get more foot cramps and need to massage your feet in a hurry?" he teased.

"Cramps can happen to anybody," Tamera said haughtily. "Even Olympic swimmers can get cramps, you know."

"Yeah, but usually not five yards from the shore," Patrick said with a grin.

Flies and mosquitoes buzzed around them as they walked.

"Ow," Tamera said, slapping at her bare shoulders. "How come they like me better than anyone else?"

"I just hope the snakes don't like you better than anyone else," Patrick said. "You're the only one with bare toes."

"Snakes?" Tamera shot Tia a worried look. "There aren't really snakes around here, are there?"

"Of course. Great big ones. Deadly poisonous ones," Patrick said, giving Tia a wink.

"Shut up," Tamera said, laughing now, too.

They left the wide trail for a narrow, rocky path.

"This goes up a little hill where there's a great view," Scott called back to them.

"A hill, what fun. That's just what I need," Tamera muttered to Tia. "My feet are killing me. And if anyone says I told you so, I'll hit them," she added.

Tia watched her hobbling along and couldn't help feeling sorry for her. Poor Tamera—she always tried so hard and she always wound up doing the wrong thing.

The path got narrower and narrower. Brambles grew on either side. Soon Tamera's legs were covered in scratches. She looked as if she had met a tiger.

"Isn't this a great view?" Tia said as they came out of the forest and stood on a rock overlooking the lake.

"Don't talk to me about views," Tamera growled. "I'm covered in mosquito bites and scratches. My feet have blisters bigger than dinner plates all over them. And I'm so pooped that I can't even breathe. All I can think of is that I've got to walk all that way down again."

She started to hobble ahead down the track.

"I guess your sister hasn't done too much hiking," Patrick said, falling into step beside Tia. "She didn't dress for it today."

"We're not exactly outdoor types," Tia said.

"I haven't done too much outdoor stuff either," Patrick said. "Just some Boy Scout camping when I was a kid. But I was a lifeguard at a country club pool all last summer. I thought a job like this might be less boring."

"I just hope I can handle it when the kids get here," Tia said. "The other counselors all seem so . . ."

"Outdoorsy? Tough? Rugged? Scary?" Patrick suggested.

He and Tia exchanged a grin. Tamera looked back and saw them.

"Guess what?" she said excitedly. "I've just seen a shortcut back to camp. We could take it and get there ahead of the others."

"Where?" Patrick asked.

"Down this slope. It's not too steep," Tamera said. "Come on, we can race the others back to camp."

"Whoa! I don't think you want to go that way," Patrick said, grabbing Tamera's arm as she stepped forward.

"Why not?"

"Because it's wall-to-wall poison ivy."

"Poison ivy? And I was about to run right through it?"

"And tomorrow you'd be one big itch," Patrick said.

"You saved my life," Tamera said, smiling at him adoringly.

Patrick was shaking his head. "I don't think I'd call you Nature Woman," he said. "And you're going to be in charge of little kids? I think you need someone watching out for you! Drowning yesterday, poison ivy today? What is it going to be tomorrow? Snakes? Quicksand?"

"Are you volunteering for the job?" Tamera teased. "If so, you could give me a piggyback to camp. My feet are killing me."

Patrick laughed. "Okay, climb on," he said.

Tia watched as Tamera climbed onto Patrick's back and they set off with squeals of laughter. How does she do it? Tia asked herself. I'm friendly and intelligent. She acts like a goofball, and she gets some guy to carry her down the hill! Tia had an uneasy feeling that when it came to fighting over boys, Tamera didn't play fair.

As they reached the bottom of the hill and Patrick set Tamera down again Roxanne caught up with them. She took one look at Tamera and raised her eyes. "What's she done this time? Broken her ankle?"

"Her feet were hurting her," Patrick said, looking embarrassed.

"She's going to be more of a pain than the campers," Roxanne said, talking as if Tamera weren't there. "You and I will have our hands full, Pat. Which reminds me—do you want to go check out that rescue equipment again? You and I need to practice working together in close cooperation, right?"

"If you say so," Patrick said.

They walked off together.

"He carried me down the hill," Tamera said, her eyes shining. "That must mean he likes me, right?"

"Or he felt sorry for you," Tia said. "Anyway, don't get your hopes up too high. Did you see the way he and Roxanne were making eye contact? She was totally flirting with him."

"So? That doesn't mean he was flirting back," Tamera said.

"He went with her willingly enough, Tamera. And she is very gorgeous."

"Then I'll have to keep on being rescued all summer," Tamera said. "Let's go find that quicksand or a few bears."

That afternoon Tia was thoughtful. Maybe she had

got things all wrong after all. Maybe guys did like girls who were goofballs and who needed protecting. She had never really gone after a guy in her life. She had had a few boyfriends, but they had just happened. Each time they had started off being friends and it had gone on from there.

But this time she was competing with Tamera and with Roxanne. Maybe she'd have to come up with a few tricks of her own!

Chapter 10

꩜

Oh no," Tamera groaned as she woke up the next Monday morning.

"What?" Tia was also instantly awake.

"The campers will be coming today. All those little kids! I just hope I don't screw up, Tia. I had dreams all night about losing kids in the wilderness."

"You'll be fine," Tia said. "We both will."

"I hope so," Tamera said. "My mind is a blank. I've forgotten everything Scott taught us." She grabbed Tia and started shaking her. "What is the Heimlich maneuver for? What do I use on beestings? I don't even know a blue jay from a sparrow."

"Tamera, let go of me," Tia said, "and stop going ballistic. You'll do fine. Like Scott said, there are trained lifeguards if you have an emergency."

"Yeah," Tamera said, a big grin spreading across

her face. "I might just have a whole bunch of emergencies and have to call you-know-who to help me."

Tia didn't say anything. It made her mad the way Tamera took it for granted that she was going to get Patrick and that he wouldn't be interested in Tia. She watched as Tamera put on her white T-shirt that said Nature Camp Counselor right across it. At least Tamera had to dress like everyone else from now on, she thought. So did Roxanne. Patrick still hadn't shown which one of them he liked best yet.

Did she still have a chance with him? Tia wondered. What chance could she possibly have if she was competing with Roxanne as well as Tamera? The problem was that she was starting to like him a lot. She loved the funny things he said to Tamera and how good-natured he was about Tamera's goof-ups. How come I have to be the smart, efficient twin? Tia asked herself. Maybe I'll have to start goofing up, too.

When Tia and Tamera got to the place where they caught the bus every morning, they found a lot of little kids waiting. Their bus was jam-packed and noisy as they rode to camp.

Around nine-thirty three more yellow school buses rolled into camp, sending up a cloud of dust behind them. They had picked up kids all around the city, and each bus had several counselors supervising the kids. As the dust cleared, Tia and Tamera watched the doors open and hordes of seven- to ten-year-olds come pouring out. They stood close together, looking around suspiciously, as if they expected to find bears behind every tree.

"Welcome to Camp Chickadee," Scott said, stepping out in front of the counselors. "I'm Scott, your camp director, and now you're going to meet your counselors. Stick with your own counselor all the time and don't wander off. That's rule number one. It's a big forest out there."

The kids looked even more nervous.

"I'm going to introduce a counselor and tell you your group name. When you hear your name called, go stand with that counselor. Got it?" He started calling out counselors and kids. Gradually the campsite filled up with little groups. Soon only Tia and Tamera were left.

"Tia," Scott called. "Your group is the Blue Jays. And the Blue Jays are going to be Alicia, Darah, Megan, Ricky, and Jared."

Tamera watched the kids join Tia. They all looked like sweet little second graders, smiling shyly at Tia. One of them even took Tia's hand. She thought Tia was lucky.

"Tamera," Scott said. "Your group is the Water Rats. Will the following campers please go to Tamera: Devon, Oliver, Rachel . . ."

A pint-size boy in torn jeans stalked over to Tamera and glared at her. He was wearing a name tag that said Devon.

"I don't want to be with no girl," he said.

"Sorry," Tamera said, not knowing what else to say.

"I didn't even want to come here," the boy went on.

"Me neither," the little girl, who had to be Rachel, added. "I'm scared of bugs."

The third little boy was gazing intensely at Tamera through heavy-framed round glasses. "My mother wouldn't let me bring most of my equipment today," he said. "I just have my basic field binoculars and my compass. But I had to leave my butterfly nets and my collecting bags at home."

Rachel grabbed Tamera's leg. "If he's collecting bugs, I'm going home."

"It'll be fine," Tamera said, trying to reassure herself as much as Rachel.

"You've only got three kids so far, Tamera," Scott said, consulting his list and glancing at the small group of kids who still had no counselor. "Who have I left out? Carmen, why don't you go to Tamera?"

A frail and scared-looking little girl walked shyly across and stood next to Rachel.

"And the last name on your list is Roger."

Tamera looked up at the mention of this name. "Roger?" she asked.

"Did somebody call me?" a voice said, and Roger came out from behind the school bus.

"Roger? What are you doing here?" Tamera asked in horror.

"I'm your newest camper, honeybun," Roger said, smiling at her sweetly. "I'm waiting for you to show me the wonders of nature."

"Roger, this is a camp for little kids. You don't

belong here. Go home," Tamera yelled. She could feel all the other counselors looking at her weirdly.

"Don't send me home, Tamera, love of my heart," Roger said. "When I found out you'd be here all summer, I just knew I had to be with you. So I lied about my age a little. I can pass for a big ten-year-old."

"No way, Roger," Tamera said. She looked appealingly at Scott. "This guy is way too old," she called. "He doesn't belong here."

"Please let me stay," Roger pleaded. "I really want to find out about the wonders of nature. I'll be helpful. I'm great with little kids. They love me. I'll do anything you want if you let me stay."

"We could use extra help," Scott said hesitantly.

"Scott!" Tamera pleaded.

"You won't regret it," Roger said, shaking Scott's hand. "I'm a whiz at keeping kids happy. Ask the kids on the bus, okay? Did I make you guys laugh?"

Several campers nodded.

"See?" Roger said.

"Okay, you can stay," Scott said. "You can be an assistant counselor and help out where you're needed, okay?"

"Thank you, thank you," Roger said. "You've made me a very happy man."

"Is he serious? He's really that desperate to learn about nature?" Patrick muttered into Tia's ear.

"No, he's desperate to be with my sister," Tia whispered back.

"That's her boyfriend?" Patrick asked.

Tia was tempted. If she told Patrick that Roger was Tamera's boyfriend, then he wouldn't be interested in Tamera anymore. But she realized that she couldn't pull a mean trick on her sister.

"He wishes," she said. "He bugs Tamera all the time, and he never gives up."

"Poor Tamera," Patrick said, smiling at Tia. "She's already got enough problems coping with the great outdoors, without having that little squirt following her around."

"That guy is Tamera's boyfriend?" Tia overheard Roxanne saying to another counselor. "It figures. Losers have to stick together, don't they? I wonder if the other sister is going to bring a dorky guy to camp with her tomorrow."

Tia glared at Roxanne's back as Roxanne led her campers toward the circle. She wanted to set her straight in a hurry, but she couldn't think of the right words to put Roxanne in her place.

"Come on, guys," she said to her campers, and followed the others to the circle. Scott went over camp rules with them. Then he taught them all "This Land Is Your Land" and a couple of funny camp songs.

"Our first activity is called Creature Count," he said when they had finished the songs. "You have fifteen minutes to explore. Stay with your group within the camp area. Your counselor will write down any creature, bird, animal, fish, or bug that you see and can identify. Ready, go."

"This is dumb," Devon said. "I want to play basketball."

"Sorry, kid, you're stuck with it," Tamera said. "Now get moving."

Devon looked surprised, then shrugged. "Okay," he said.

"I can already hear an acorn woodpecker," Oliver said.

"You have to see it first," Rachel insisted.

"He heard it. That's good enough. Put it down," Devon said. "What else do you hear, four-eyes?"

"Hey, that's not nice, Devon," Tamera said. "You wouldn't like it if he called you squirt or shrimp, would you?"

"People do all the time," Devon said.

"And does it make you feel good?" Tamera insisted.

"No," Devon conceded.

"There you are then," Tamera said.

By the end of fifteen minutes they had a long list, and even Rachel and Devon had gotten into the activity, even though they weren't much help in identifying anything.

Meanwhile Tia was having problems.

"I have to go to the bathroom," one of the little girls said.

"Me too," the other girls agreed.

"Okay, I'll show you where it is," Tia said, leading them across to the rest rooms.

The girls went inside, then came running out, screaming, "There's a big spider on the door!"

Tia hated spiders. She had to force herself to go inside. "I'm sure it's only a little—" she said. Then she stopped. It wasn't little. It was big and black, and it was sitting right next to the door handle leading to the toilet. She swallowed hard.

"Kill it," Darah insisted.

"No, Darah. We don't kill things at nature camp. This is their territory," Tia said.

"Then take it off the door," Darah said.

Tia prayed that anyone, even Roxanne, would come into the bathroom.

"Maybe we could get a box or a jar to put it in," she suggested.

"Hurry up, you guys, we're losing the game," the boys in her group yelled through the bathroom door. Tia wondered if the boys would be able to touch a spider without freaking out and if she could bring them into the girl's bathroom.

"I've got the cup from my thermos bottle in my lunch box," Alicia said. She ran to get it and handed it to Tia. It was a very small cup. How quickly could a spider run up the side of it and onto her arm?

Tia closed her eyes and put the cup over the spider. She opened them enough to see wiggling legs in the bottom of the cup. She sprinted outside and tipped the spider into the nearest bush.

By the time the last girl had used the bathroom, Scott called time. Tia still felt sick as they got into a circle again.

"How many creatures, Tia?" Scott asked as he finally got to Tia's group.

"One," her campers said in disgust.

"Only one?" Scott sounded as if he couldn't believe what he was hearing.

"Yeah. A spider. It trapped us in the bathroom, and we don't even know what kind," Darah added.

The other kids burst into noisy laughter. Even the other counselors were smiling.

"How many, Tamera?" Scott asked quickly, trying to regain control.

"Fifty-four," Tamera said.

"Including a rare sighting of a dragonfly nymph," Oliver added for her.

"Good job, Water Rats," Scott said. "You're clearly the winners."

Devon and Oliver gave each other high fives. Tamera grinned. Maybe her kids weren't such losers after all. For once she had beaten Tia.

"You only found one thing?" she couldn't help asking Tia. "What happened to the person who could identify every bug north of Florida, huh?"

Tia frowned at her. "I got trapped in the bathroom by a spider, okay?"

"A black widow? A tarantula?" Tamera asked.

"No, just a big, fat, horrible spider. Now leave me alone," Tia said, and she pushed past Tamera and walked away.

Chapter 11

Tia didn't stop feeling bad all morning. She saw Roxanne looking in her direction and giggling with one of the other counselors. Tia was sure they were giggling about her and the spider. And worse still, her campers didn't think she was a hero for finally getting rid of the spider. They thought she was a wimp because she hadn't killed it right away.

Before lunch it was her group's turn to try the canoes. As she put her campers into life vests, Patrick came over to her.

"If it makes you feel better, I hate spiders, too," he whispered.

"You do?" Tia looked up at him. His eyes were warm as he smiled down at her.

"Yeah. I don't think I like any kind of bugs," he said. "That's why I'm glad I'm stuck here, around the water." He leaned closer to her. "What part of the city do you live in, Tia? I just wondered if—"

A loud scream made them both jump. Tamera came rushing down the slope, followed by her campers.

"There's a bear up there," she yelled.

"A bear? Where?" Patrick asked.

"Up there in the trees. I saw it crashing around, and it's coming this way!"

"We're all going to get eaten," Rachel whimpered, grabbing Tamera's leg.

"I really don't think . . ." Oliver began, but nobody was listening. Patrick led the way as they all hurried to where Tamera was pointing.

"If there is a bear, we'd better get a ranger," Patrick said. "Where did you think you saw it?"

"Over there," Tamera said. "A big black bear, crashing through the forest. Look, there it is now! Quick, run. Climb a tree or something."

"Tamera," Patrick said as she tried to run off. "That's not a bear."

"It's not?"

"No, Tamera," Tia said triumphantly. "It's a dog."

A big black shaggy animal came bounding up to the campers and started licking them. Immediately an elderly man in hiking gear came hurrying down the trail toward them.

"Oh, thank you, you found my dog," he said. "He's not supposed to be in a nature preserve, but I stopped for a moment and he jumped out of the car.

Bad boy, Kelsey." He led the friendly dog back up the trail.

Everyone turned to look at Tamera.

"It sure looked like a bear to me," Tamera said.

"There are no bears here," Oliver said scathingly. "I kept trying to tell you that."

"Sorry," Tamera said, grinning sheepishly. "Oh well, time for canoes, right?"

Tia watched her sister as they headed back to the beach. A weird thought was nagging at the back of her mind. Had Tamera really believed she had seen a bear, or had she seen Tia and Patrick together and wanted to get Patrick's attention again? Tia was sure he was about to ask her on a date when Tamera had screamed.

I'm just imagining things, Tia told herself, but the bad feeling wouldn't go away. She sat on her bed that evening and watched Tamera brushing her hair. Was it possible that Tamera was acting helpless to get Patrick to notice her? She knew that Tamera wasn't above playing dirty tricks—she had already tried a fake drowning. It was so unfair, Tia decided. It really seemed that Patrick liked her, and yet they never got a chance to be together because Tamera was always there.

Tomorrow night was the counselors' campfire. They were going to stay late at the lake and have a cookout and campfire skits.

"Have you come up with a skit yet for tomorrow's campfire?" she asked Tamera.

"No, have you?"

"Not really," Tia said. "I guess we missed out by not being Girl Scouts. I think I'll ask my mom if she's got any ideas."

"And I could ask my dad. He was a Boy Scout," Tamera said.

Tia went downstairs to find Lisa. Tamera went to find Ray.

Lisa was sitting at the kitchen table, finishing a carton of ice cream with a soup spoon.

"This needed eating up in a hurry before it went bad," she said defensively when she saw Tia. "You want some? I'm a nice person. I can share."

"No thanks, Mom," Tia said, smiling. "I need your help. I have to do a skit for a campfire tomorrow. I've never even been to a campfire. Got any ideas?"

Lisa stopped scooping ice cream and thought for a moment. "Campfire skit, huh? It's years since I saw a campfire. But I remember one thing I saw once that was cute," she said. "You kneel down and put your hands into a pair of shoes. Then another person puts on a big jacket and hides behind you and together you make one little person. The other person is the arms and you are the head and feet and you do a dance or something."

"That sounds like fun," Tia said. "I wonder if Tamera would do it with me."

She ran back upstairs and waited until Tamera came back to the bedroom. "Hey, Tamera, do you want to do a skit with me?" she asked.

Tamera shook her head. "Sorry, I've come up with a great idea of my own that takes two people. And you know what I was thinking? I think I'll ask Patrick to do it with me."

"You're going to ask Patrick?" Tia blurted out.

"Sure, why not? It's a free country, isn't it?"

"Tamera, why don't you give it up," Tia said. "It's obvious he likes me better."

"Obvious? To whom? Not to me," Tamera said. "Look how quickly he came running to save me when he thought I'd found a bear. And he carried me down the hill when my feet hurt me. Guys don't offer to give a girl a piggyback ride unless they are definitely interested."

"He didn't offer," Tia said. "You forced him into it."

"I did not!"

"Did, too!"

"You're just jealous because he likes me better," Tamera said.

"He does not!" Tia shouted.

"We'll see," Tamera said. "When he and I have time to work on our skit together in the dark by the campfire."

Tia got into bed and pulled the covers over her head. Why hadn't she thought of asking Patrick to help her with her skit? She still could, she told herself. He could be the second person for her dance. She imagined what it would be like to have Patrick close to her like that, sharing a jacket with him, his arms around her. She made up her mind to ask him the next morning.

*　　*　　*

The next day Tia was busy from the moment her bus arrived at camp. First they went on a field trip, making plaster casts of paw prints they found on the trails and lake shore. By the end of the morning they had rabbits and raccoons and even a fox, as well as several bird species. At lunchtime they made happy-face sandwiches and instant pudding with the kids. After lunch an arts and crafts counselor came to show them how to make animal masks. It wasn't until the campers were bused home and the counselors started to get ready for the campfire that she managed to talk to Patrick alone.

"I was wondering if you'd help me with my skit," Tia said shyly.

Patrick's face clouded. "I would have loved to, Tia, but I already promised Tamera," he said. "The thing she wants to do is quite complicated, so I told her we'd rehearse now." He looked at Tia's face. "I'm really sorry," he said. "I wish I could help you, but Tamera did ask me first."

"It's okay," Tia managed to say with a bright smile. "I'll get someone else."

"Did I hear you mention that you needed help?" Roger asked, appearing beside her. "I just volunteered to help Tamera, but she turned me down, so here I am—ready, willing, and able."

"Okay, Roger, I guess you'll have to do," Tia said with a sigh. She started explaining how they were going to do the skit.

It was getting dark by the time they had finished eating hot dogs and beans. Scott got out his guitar, and they sang together around the campfire. Then they started the skits.

"I hope you take note of all the good skits so that you can do them with your kids when we have a group campfire," Scott said. "Now, who would like to go first?"

"I would," Tamera said, waving her hand. "Patrick and I have a great skit."

"Okay, Tamera. You're up then," Scott said.

"We need a couple of seconds to get ready," Tamera said. She and Patrick disappeared. Then Tamera appeared again at the edge of the circle. She was wearing a man's hat and a big jacket and she was on her knees with her hands in a big pair of shoes. She had various bowls and jugs in front of her. Then she started a skit about getting the dinner. Of course it was Patrick's arms in the jacket and he couldn't see what he was doing. Tamera said, "Now I'm going to pour the milk," and Patrick poured and missed the glass completely.

"I think I'll have some of this delicious pudding," Tamera said. Patrick's hand, holding the spoon, came up to Tamera's face and missed her mouth. Tamera got pudding all over her cheeks. The other counselors were howling with laughter.

Tia sat there, feeling that she was about to explode. Not only had Tamera stolen her idea, but she had made it way better and funnier than Tia's. There was no way she could even do hers now.

The skit ended to loud applause. Patrick appeared from under the jacket. "Sorry about your face," he said as he noticed the pudding all over Tamera's cheeks. He put his hand up and gently scraped the pudding from her cheek. "Mmmm, butterscotch, my favorite," he said as he licked his fingers, his eyes teasing hers. Tamera gazed up at him adoringly as they disappeared from the circle, laughing together.

Tia didn't know what to do. She sat there, with angry thoughts buzzing around inside her head. When Scott called on her she said that she didn't have a skit.

"What do you mean?" Roger asked. "You're not going to do your skit now?"

"How can I?" Tia said bitterly. "Tamera just did it. Everyone will think I copied her."

She noticed Tamera, across the circle, looking at her questioningly. Tia looked away.

The moment the skits were over she fought her way across to Tamera.

"What happened to your skit?" Tamera asked innocently.

"As if you didn't know, traitor," Tia snapped.

"What are you talking about?"

"You stole my skit," Tia said. "You pretended to go ask your father, but instead you snooped on my mom and me and you stole my idea."

"I did not!" Tamera said angrily. "If you want to know, my dad gave me my idea."

"Oh, right," Tia said. "You expect me to believe that your dad came up with exactly the same idea as my mom? Give me a break, Tamera. You'd do anything to get Patrick away from me, wouldn't you, even steal from your own sister."

"How can I get Patrick away from you when he was never with you, huh?" Tamera demanded. "You're just a sore loser because Patrick thinks I'm fun and he likes me better."

"How can he ever have a chance to know if he likes me if you're always butting in, acting like a total idiot and stealing my ideas?" Tia yelled.

"You know what your problem is, don't you?" Tamera began.

Tia looked up. The other counselors were standing there, watching them. She saw Patrick's confused face, Roxanne's amused one.

"Stay away from me. I'm not talking to you anymore," Tia muttered, and she started to walk away.

"Two can play that game, Tia Landry," Tamera called after her. "I'm not talking to you, either."

Chapter 12

∞

*T*ia and Tamera sat in separate seats all the way home. Tia was feeling so mad that she even let Roger sit beside her. That evening she managed to keep out of Tamera's way at home so that Ray and Lisa didn't notice anything was wrong. But she felt scared and empty inside. She and Tamera hardly ever had big fights.

A whole day of camp went by and still Tia and Tamera weren't talking.

"What's with you and Tamera?" Denise asked her on Thursday morning at camp. "You're avoiding each other like the plague."

"We're not talking to each other," Tia said. "She stole my skit idea."

"That's it?" Denise asked. "You're not talking to each other just because she stole your idea for a crummy skit?"

"It's not just that," Tia said. "That was the last straw. We both like Patrick, you see, and I've been playing fair and she hasn't. She's pulled all sorts of stunts to make him notice her—you know, fake drowning, getting him to carry her, screaming that a bear was coming after her, and then taking my skit and doing it with him. It's not fair, Denise."

"I don't know why you're so worried," Denise said. "They didn't work, did they? It seems to me that Patrick is still equally friendly with all the girls."

"I guess," Tia said. "It's just that I thought . . ." she broke off, embarrassed. "I thought he was interested in me. He almost asked me out, only Tamera got his attention away. Since the campfire night he's just been friendly, nothing more."

"I think Patrick is just a friendly guy," Denise said. "And you've got stiff competition too. Roxanne has been calling him at home. I heard her telling her friend Joanie. And she said something about going to a movie with him."

"How can he like Roxanne?" Tia sighed. "She thinks so much of herself."

"Maybe because she's so gorgeous?" Denise suggested. "Let's face it, Tia. When it comes to great brains, great personalities, or great looks, guys go for great looks. If you hear her talking to her friends, she and Patrick are practically an item."

Tia nodded. "You're right. I guess it was always hopeless."

"So maybe you and Tamera should make up. It's dumb to stay mad at each other."

Tia looked across at Tamera, who was helping her campers to launch a canoe. Tamera was waving her arms and making them all laugh. She looked so funny that Tia's heart began to melt. Maybe Denise was right. It was dumb to stay mad at her sister because they were rivals over a guy. Especially if the guy didn't like either of them.

"Are you ready for the Find the Flags contest after lunch?" Denise asked.

"I hope so," Tia said. "I don't exactly have the gutsiest group of campers. They cling to my legs every time we have to go into the trees. And they always complain that they're tired and they want to go home. And they're freaked out by every bug."

"I think that's true for most of the kids here," Denise said, grinning. "This is all so new to most of them. But it's great to watch how they gradually get more confident, isn't it?"

As Tia walked away, she felt guilty. She had been so wrapped up in her fight with Tamera that she hadn't stopped to think about her campers. Denise was right—helping them to have a great first experience in the outdoors should be her number one priority now. She made up her mind to stop worrying about Tamera and Patrick and Roxanne. She was going to help her campers learn to feel good about themselves. Maybe they'd even win the Find the Flags contest that afternoon!

As soon as the campers had finished lunch, Scott had them all sit together in the circle.

"This is serious stuff," he said to them. "This is

your first real adventure in the wilderness. You've learned a lot already in the few days you've been here. Now you're going to put it into practice."

He handed out sheets of paper to all the counselors. "Here's how we play the game," he said. "What you have there is a blank map, plus a list of instructions to take you through the forest. Along the way you'll find little colored flags at each of the twelve checkpoints. Take one flag from each checkpoint. First team back with all twelve wins."

Tia looked down at her instruction sheet. At the top of it was a primitive map with instructions written underneath. "First flag one hundred paces due east of the big white oak tree." The instructions were a combination of compass directions and recognizing various trees, rocks, and shrubs.

"You can find your flags in any order you want," Scott said, "and I want you all back here by three o'clock, even if you haven't found them all. Any questions?"

"Yeah, do we have to do this?" Devon demanded.

"What if we meet a bear?" Rachel whimpered.

"I want to go home now," another little voice came from the crowd.

"Hey, this is going to be fun, guys," Scott said. "Imagine that you're real pioneers. Okay, ready, set, go!"

Tia took off with her group along a shady path. It wasn't hard to follow the map. Other groups were ahead of her, and she could hear by their excited yells that they had found flags. Soon her group had four.

This was great, she thought. They might have a chance at winning.

"I've got a rock in my shoe," Darah complained, and flopped down onto a rock. By the time Tia had helped her take off her sneaker and put it on again the forest around them was silent.

"Come on, guys, we've got to catch up," she said. She hurried them down the path until they came to a fork.

"Which way do we go now?" Ricky asked, glancing at Tia's map.

"I'm not sure," Tia said. She had been so confident, following other groups, that she wasn't even sure which path they had started out on. So she wasn't one hundred percent sure which flags they had already found. She paused and listened. She thought she could hear voices over to the right.

"This one," she said.

After what seemed like at least an hour of walking, they hadn't found another flag, or heard any more voices.

"Where are we?" Alicia asked.

"Are we lost?" Darah added.

"My feet hurt me."

"I'm tired. I don't want to walk anymore."

"Let's go back to camp."

The campers sank down onto a boulder.

Tia bit her lip. She didn't want to admit they might be lost.

"I'm sure we're fine," she said. She looked around hopefully. The trees were so thick here that it was impossible to spot landmarks in the distance. And the sun had already sunk behind the trees, so she couldn't even tell where west was.

"Listen," she said, smiling happily. "I can hear voices. Someone's coming this way. See, I told you we were okay."

Tamera had started off in the opposite direction from Tia. She was keeping as far away from Tia as possible since Tia had turned so mean to her. She had never known Tia to be so jealous before, or so unfair.

I didn't even do anything wrong, Tamera told herself. She'd tried to set things right, but Tia wouldn't even give her a chance to explain.

Tamera stomped along the forest paths, her head full of angry thoughts, not really paying too much attention to which path she was taking. After a while she glanced down at her map. "We're doing great, guys," she said to her campers. "We turned right at the big elm tree it mentions."

"That wasn't an elm. It was a beech," Oliver said dryly.

"Are you sure?" Tamera asked.

"That great big tree where we turned right? It was a beech," Oliver said.

"Then why didn't you say something?" Tamera snapped.

"I thought you knew what we were doing," Oliver said.

"Okay, Mr. Know-It-All," Tamera said. "You tell us which way we should be going now."

"Unfortunately I didn't bring my compass today," Oliver said.

"Are we lost?" Devon demanded. "See, I knew girls couldn't read maps."

"Girls can read maps," Tamera said coldly. "Just not this girl," she added under her breath.

"Then where are we?" Devon asked, peering at the instruction sheet.

"I think we're about here," Tamera said, pointing hopefully somewhere in the middle of the map.

"Then there should be a flag hidden in a hollow tree down this path," Oliver said. He started off ahead of the others. The path twisted and turned, and they didn't find a hollow tree.

"I don't think you were right about our position on the map," Oliver said.

"We're lost, aren't we?" Devon said again. "I knew it. We'll be here all night."

"We'll die of starvation," Rachel wailed. "Or we'll freeze to death."

"We'll be okay. We can catch squirrels and skin them and roast them," Devon said.

"Euwww," Carmen and Rachel wailed, grabbing each other.

"I have to point out that I didn't bring my matches today," Oliver said. "So our chances of making a fire are pretty small."

"We could use your glasses, dummy," Devon said.

"Not if the sun has gone behind clouds, which it has," Oliver said.

"Come on, guys, we'll be fine," Tamera said. "How far from camp can we be?" She decided not to try for any more flags but to make it safely back to camp. She glanced at her watch. Two-thirty. They were supposed to be back by three.

She headed down a wide path, ahead of her campers. She could see footprints in the sand. This path had been used recently. All she had to do was follow it and she'd be fine. She came around a corner and there was Tia, sitting on a rock with her campers.

"Oh, hi," Tamera said guardedly.

"Hi," Tia said, getting up. "Boy, am I glad to see you."

"Don't tell me you were lost?" Tamera asked, a grin spreading across her face. "The person who knew every bug and tree and flower from here to Mexico is lost?"

"No, just resting," Tia said quickly. "We're not lost. You're not lost, are you?"

"No, just heading back to camp."

"Good, then we'll come with you. We've rested long enough," Tia said.

"We are too lost," Darah said before Tia could shut her up.

"Hah!" Tamera said. "I knew it."

"We're lost, too," Rachel said. "We thought we'd have to spend the night in the woods, and the wolves and bears would get us."

Tia and Tamera looked at each other.

"Okay, so we were having a few problems," Tamera admitted.

"We were, too," Tia said. "But now that you're here, we can figure things out together."

"Sure we can," Tamera said. "You're the smart one. You should be able to figure out this map."

They spread the map out on the rock.

"Where was the last point on the map that you positively knew where you were?" Tamera asked.

"I'm not sure," Tia said.

"Great. Now we're all lost together," Devon said. "We'll probably be out here for weeks, and we'll have to start eating each other if we can't catch squirrels."

Rachel and Carmen let out horrified wails.

"Devon, cool it," Tamera said.

"Let's work this out scientifically," Tia said. "The sun is behind us, right? Then our camp must be to the east, which is over there."

Both groups started walking down the trail. The path looked promising to start with, but then it got narrower and more twisting. Brambles grew across it. The kids started to cry as they got scratched.

"Be brave, it's not much longer," Tamera called out. They pushed through the last of the brambles. "I'm sure I've seen this place before," Tamera said.

"Yeah, it's the rock we were sitting on half an hour ago," Ricky said dryly. "We've come in a big circle."

Rachel started to cry. "We'll never get out," she said. "We're trapped here forever and ever. It's a magic forest, I know it. Any minute now the monsters will come out and get us."

Carmen started to cry, too.

Tia took Tamera's arm and led her aside. "We can't keep walking around in circles like this," she said. "The kids are getting really tired."

Tamera looked around. "Tell you what," she said. "You stay here and I'll go looking for signs of the others. All the rest of the groups are out here somewhere."

"If they haven't all finished by now and gotten back to camp."

"They can't all have finished," Tamera said. "I'll try to find a path with lots of footprints on it and that will take us back to camp."

"Don't you get lost," Tia said.

"Here, take my pocketknife," Oliver said. "You can mark the trees as you go."

"Good idea," Tamera said. "I'll be back soon."

She hurried down the trail, her heart beating very fast. Then she stopped. Something was coming through the woods toward her, something big and dark, crashing through the undergrowth. Oliver had said there were no bears here, but was he always right?

Then suddenly the creature burst out onto the trail. Tamera opened her mouth to scream.

"You're safe now, my little flower. I've found you," Roger said.

Chapter 13

❧

Roger! What are you doing here?" Tamera gasped.

"Looking for you, love of my life," Roger said, smiling at her fondly. "When you didn't come back to camp, I thought that maybe something terrible had happened to you, so I came to find you. And here I am"

"Don't tell me you know the way back to camp?" Tamera asked.

"Of course. It's just down that trail and turn left at the holly bush. I took a shortcut."

"Roger, I know I'm going to regret saying this, but I'm really glad to see you," Tamera said.

"So you were lost? My instinct said you were in trouble. My instinct never lies where you are concerned. That little red light goes off in my brain and I leap to save you, like Superman!" Tamera tried not to smile. "But don't worry, you're safe now, I'll lead you all safely back." He looked around. "Where are your campers? You didn't lose them, did you?"

"No, they're back there with Tia. She was lost, too."

"Then let's go get them," Roger said.

A crazy idea was forming in Tamera's head. She remembered all the times that Tia had been the smart one—Tia learning the names of all the animals before anyone else, Tia getting science awards. Ever since Tia had come to live with Tamera, it had been Tia who did everything right and got all the praise. Tia was so sure of herself that she hadn't believed her own sister. Now Tamera had a chance to get even.

"Roger, I might regret this later, too, but I'm going to ask you to do a big favor for me."

"What's in it for me?" Roger asked.

Tamera took a deep breath and swallowed hard. "I'll . . . I'll go on a date with you," she said.

"All right!" Roger said. "You name it, I'll do it."

"I want you to go ahead of me back to camp. Take this knife and mark the trees as you go so that I can follow you."

"Okay," Roger said suspiciously. "Any particular reason for this?"

Tamera found it hard to tell him the truth. "I'd, uh, like my campers to think I found the way back to camp, not that I had to be rescued. They think I'm pretty lame."

"I understand," Roger said. "Think nothing of it. I'll be happy to do it for you. I'll make a little nick on the trees, like this. That's easy enough to see. Hurry back, my little flower, so we can start planning our date together."

"Oh, and Roger," Tamera called after him. "Breathe one word about our date to anyone at camp, and you're dead meat."

She hurried back to Tia. The campers looked up hopefully as she ran into the clearing.

"Okay, guys, everything's fine," she said. "Just follow me."

"You found the way back to camp? So quickly?" Tia asked.

Tamera nodded. "It wasn't hard."

"Hooray. We're not going to be eaten by bears or monsters," Rachel said.

"I keep telling you there are no bears," Oliver said. "And no monsters."

"Oliver, shut up," Devon said.

Tamera led them confidently down the trail. The marks on the trees were easy to spot.

Behind her the kids started singing as they marched.

"Tamera, I'm really impressed," Tia said. "This could have been so embarrassing. We could have gotten into all kinds of trouble. We could have been fired again, but you saved us. I'm sorry about the things I said to you."

"That's okay," Tamera said. "I guess it's nice to know that dumb people have their uses sometimes."

"You're not dumb, Tamera. I never thought you

were dumb," Tia said. "A goofball sometimes, but never dumb."

"Here they are now," someone yelled as the two groups emerged at the campsite.

"Good going, girls," Scott said. "We were getting worried about you. The buses are ready to leave. I was about to send out search parties."

"We sort of got lost for a while," Tamera said. "But we handled it okay."

"You know," Scott said, "I was feeling guilty because you guys didn't get as much training as the rest of the counselors, but you did great."

"Tamera did it," Tia said. "She was the one who found the way back for us. She was terrific."

Tamera smiled modestly. "I just used all the outdoor skills you taught us. It was simple really."

Patrick came up to them. "I was all set to volunteer for the search party," he said. "I thought you might need another piggyback ride."

Tamera smiled up at him. "No, but I could use another tuna fish sandwich," she said. "Being a hero makes me hungry."

"I think I've still got some lunch left," Patrick said. "I'll go find my backpack."

"He's gone to find his backpack. Isn't that sweet?" Tamera asked Tia. "And did you see how worried he was that we were lost? He really is the sweetest guy."

She broke off as Roger came up to her. "So I guess I made good marks that you could follow, right?"

"Marks, what marks?" Tia asked.

"Marks, uh, on the lawn at home," Tamera started

to say, but Roger said, "The marks on the trees, so that she could find her way back." He handed over Oliver's pocketknife.

'You made marks on the trees for her?" Tia demanded. "She didn't find her own way back?"

"Whoops. Did I say something I shouldn't?" Roger asked.

"No, Roger, you just blew the whole thing," Tamera said.

Tia was glaring at her. "You cheated again, didn't you? Is there anything in the world you can do without cheating? You had Roger show you the way back? How low can you sink, Tamera?"

She stormed off, leaving Tamera looking after her.

'You can forget about that date, Roger," Tamera said.

On Friday the campers' week was going to finish with a big water carnival. All morning long they practiced for the events, the canoe race, crazy swimming relays, and the watermelon-eating contest. Tamera was trying not to think about her fight with Tia. Her campers were looking good for the canoe race. Pint-size Devon and frail-looking little Carmen could really paddle. Even Rachel and Oliver weren't too bad, and Tamera found that paddling was something that came naturally to her.

"I think we're going to kick butt," Devon said as they pulled up their canoe after morning practice. "Did you see how we overtook those other guys?"

"You're really good, Devon," Rachel said admiringly.

"So is Carmen," Oliver said.

"Yeah, she's not bad, for a girl," Devon admitted. "Neither is Tamera. She's got muscles like a guy."

"I don't know if that's a compliment or not, Devon," Tamera said.

They went up from the beach to get their lunchboxes, then they met at the picnic tables.

"Make sure you eat lots of good stuff for energy and not junk food," Tamera said. "Especially—" She looked around. "Where's Devon?" she asked.

"Roxanne wanted to talk to him," Rachel said.

"Roxanne? What can she want with Devon?" Tamera asked.

At last Devon came running up to them, out of breath. He sat at the table and opened his lunchbox.

"What did Roxanne want?" Tamera asked.

Devon started to sip his juice. "She wanted me to join her team for the canoe race," he said.

"She did what?" Tamera demanded.

"She said we'd have the winning team and I'd win a medal if I was with them."

"Boy, does she have a nerve," Tamera said.

Devon went on looking down at his lunch. "She said she was one of the head guys, so she could pick who she wanted."

There was a tense silence. Devon started to eat his sandwich.

"You didn't say yes, did you?" Tamera asked.

Devon shrugged. "It would be nice to get a medal," he said. "I never got a medal."

"*We've* got a chance for a medal," Tamera said.

"Not if Roxanne picks the best kids from the whole camp."

Tamera nodded. This was true. "Okay, Devon. It's up to you," she said. "You have to do what you think is right."

"And if you join Roxanne, then you stink," Rachel said.

"No, Rachel. We have to let Devon make up his own mind," Tamera said "If he joins Roxanne, then we'll do our best without him."

"But it won't be so good," Carmen said.

They finished eating. Nobody said much. Tamera watched Roxanne head down to the beach. A little while later Devon got up and followed her. He didn't show up as they joined the rest of the campers to watch the first events.

If Tamera hadn't been feeling so bad, the relays would have been fun to watch. There was a T-shirt relay where the teams had to put wet T-shirts on each other before it was their turn to swim. Then there was an inner-tube relay and one blowing a Ping-Pong ball in front of the swimmers.

Tamera's team didn't enter any of the swim relays. Two of her campers couldn't even swim, and the other two could only manage the doggy paddle. But Tia had some great swimmers. Her team won the Ping-Pong relay. Tamera really wanted to root for Tia's team, but she didn't want Tia to see her cheering. She could see Devon's head close to Roxanne down the beach. It looked as if she had lost her sister *and* her best paddler.

Then Scott announced the canoe race. They had to paddle out around a buoy and then back to the beach. As Tamera helped her team launch their canoe, Devon came running over to them.

"Okay, what are we waiting for? Let's get this boat in the water," Devon yelled.

"What happened to Roxanne?" Tamera asked.

"I told her to get lost," Devon said. "She said some mean things about you. She said you and Tia were losers." Devon frowned as he used all his strength to push the boat into the water.

"We'll show her, won't we guys?" Tamera said.

At that moment Roxanne walked past. "Surely you aren't entering the canoe race?" she asked, breaking into phony giggles. "I'd quit now, before you embarrass yourselves. Big mistake, Devon," she added as she went to her own canoe.

Tamera looked across. Roxanne really had taken all the best kids for her team. And in the back of the boat was Roger.

"What's he doing there?" she demanded.

Roxanne grinned. "He signed up as a camper, didn't he? I'm just using names from the official list."

"Roger, get out of that boat right now," Tamera said. "It's not fair if her team has two counselors in it."

"All's fair in love and war, honeybun," Roger said.

"You canceled our date, after I did something nice for you, remember?"

"Don't ever come near me again, Roger," Tamera said. She turned back to her team. "Make sure you put your life jackets on properly," she said, and went around checking them.

"Where's your jacket?" Carmen asked.

"It's right . . ." Tamera looked around. "It was here a few moments ago."

She started searching around the canoe.

"Okay, everyone in the canoes," Scott called.

Tamera got in without her jacket.

"Ready, set, go!" Scott yelled.

Tamera's team started paddling furiously. The canoe shot across the water. Tamera's arms were pumping as if she were a machine. She peeked across and saw that they were already up on most of the canoes. Only Roxanne's canoe of all-stars was even with them.

"Come on, guys, we can do this," Tamera urged.

She could hear the cheers and yells echoing from the shore. The buoy was ahead of them. If she put on an extra spurt of energy, her group would be first to turn and ahead of Roxanne's team.

The buoy came up. Tamera dug in her paddle on the left side of the boat to swing it around. One moment they were skimming across the water, the next moment the canoe tipped over with Tamera under it.

Chapter 14

༺༒༻

*T*ia had been watching the canoe race from the shore. She was still very mad at Tamera, but it was hard not to cheer for her as her boat inched ahead of Roxanne's. Tamera was first around the buoy. Tia noticed that most of the campers were yelling, "Go, Tamera." There were almost no "Go, Roxannes" echoing across the lake.

Then suddenly Tamera's canoe flipped. Tia jumped to her feet. Four little heads bobbed to the surface. Tia could see their bright orange life vests holding them up. The canoe floated upside down, and there was no sign of Tamera.

Tia didn't stop to think. She was already wearing her bathing suit. She sprinted into the water and started swimming. She knew she wasn't the world's greatest swimmer, but she had to get to Tamera.

Please let her be okay, she found herself praying. She knew that she couldn't live without Tamera. However annoying Tamera was sometimes, she was her sister and she loved her more than anyone in the world.

Tia had never swum so fast before. When she reached the canoe she was gasping for breath.

"Tamera!" she yelled with all her strength.

"Under here," came a voice.

Tia ducked under the water. Tamera was under the upside-down canoe, her face above the water line, clinging to one of the seats.

"You nearly scared me to death," Tia said. "What are you doing in here?"

"I was scared to swim out," Tamera said. "You know I get water up my nose when I try to swim underwater."

"You crazy idiot," Tia said, half laughing, half crying. "I was scared you'd drowned."

"I didn't think you'd care," Tamera said.

"Of course I care about you, dummy," Tia said. "I realized that when you didn't come up. We might fight sometimes, but you're my twin. How could I live without you?"

"I feel the same way," Tamera said. "I'd like to hug you now, but I can't let go of this seat."

"Come on, take my hand," Tia said. "You'll be fine,"

"I don't think I can let go, Tia," Tamera said, the panic rising in her voice.

"You can do it. Close your eyes, hold your breath, and take my hand."

At that moment there was the sound of splashing and Patrick's head appeared beside them. "How come you guys are having a party and didn't invite me?" he said. He was laughing, but he looked scared, too.

"Did you bring the chips with you?" Tamera asked, laughing shakily.

"No, but there's plenty to drink around here," he said. He looked at Tamera. "You spend your life freaking me out, don't you? I was helping bring the little kids in to shore, and then I realized that I couldn't see you. I must have broken the freestyle record swimming back to you."

Tia noticed the way he was looking at Tamera. He really does like her, she thought. She was about to tell him that Tamera was scared to get her face wet. But she swallowed back the words. She wasn't going to try to score points over Tamera anymore. If Patrick liked Tamera better, then she wasn't going to stand in her way.

Tamera gave Patrick an embarrassed grin. "I'm not much of a swimmer," she said. "I don't like getting my face wet."

"That's okay," Patrick said. "Tia and I will have you out in a second. Hold your breath. Ready. Go!"

Tia took Tamera's arm, and they swam with her under the canoe and up to the surface.

"Hey, that wasn't so bad," Tamera said when they

reached shallow water and could stand. "All I need is a few swimming lessons. Any volunteers?"

Patrick was smiling at her. "Sure. Any time," he said.

"Help! Help!" A voice echoed across the water.

"Looks like someone really does need you, Mr. Lifeguard," Tamera said, pointing at a thrashing figure, clinging to the buoy.

"Oh my gosh, it's Roger," Tia yelled.

"Roger, what are you doing now?" Tamera shouted to him.

"I jumped out of my boat to save you," Roger yelled back. "Then I remembered that I can't swim."

"And Roxanne just left him," Patrick commented. They all turned to see Roxanne's canoe, already on the beach. "Some lifeguard she is."

He swam across to Roger and was soon towing him back with easy strokes. Brandon and Denise came out into the water to help bring him up onto the beach.

"I thought you liked Roxanne," Tamera said to Patrick. "At least, she thought you did."

"Roxanne?" Patrick wrinkled his nose. "No way, José. She's too pushy. I hate pushy girls. I like to help maidens in distress and feel like a hero." He gave Tamera a special smile.

"That's okay. I'll leave you two alone," Tia said, and started to walk up onto the beach beside the spluttering Roger.

"No, Tia, wait," Patrick called after her. "Don't go."

"So you like her better? I knew it," Tamera said. "That's okay. I'll be a good loser."

"That's been my problem all along," he said. "I couldn't decide which one of you I like better, and I didn't want to offend the other one. There were so many times when I was about to ask one of you on a date, and then the other one showed up and I told myself I couldn't choose between you. You're so alike."

"Alike?" Tia and Tamera said at the same time. "We're totally different."

"But you look alike. You sound alike."

"I don't like tuna fish sandwiches, and she does," Tia said.

Patrick laughed, then he grew solemn again. "And I could see that I was only causing problems between you," he said. "So I thought I'd just stay friends with both of you."

"Friends is good," Tia said. "I'd like to be friends with you, Patrick."

"Me, too," Tamera said.

"Yeah, I wouldn't want to come between you and your boyfriend there," Patrick said with a wicked grin. He nodded to Roger, who was coughing violently as he was attended to by Scott and the other counselors.

"He jumped in to save me," Tamera said, looking at Roger fondly. "He's really a sweet little guy." She realized what she had said and glared at Tia. "And if you ever tell him that, I really won't speak to you for a year!"

Scott came to meet them as they stepped onto the beach.

"Nice rescue work, guys," he said. "I'm glad you're okay, Tamera. It was dumb to go out there without a life vest."

"My life vest disappeared," Tamera said. "And I didn't want to let my team down. I guess Roxanne's team won after all."

She looked down the beach. Roxanne was walking around with a big medal around her neck. A horrible suspicion was nagging at the back of Tamera's mind. She knew that life vest had been there moments before. Had Roxanne hidden it to stop her from winning the race? Then she went one step further. She remembered how easily the canoe had flipped. Had Roxanne done something to her canoe? She had gone alone to the beach at lunchtime, hadn't she?

A couple of the counselors had swum out to bring in the canoe.

"Here," Tia said, and wrapped Tamera in a towel. "Are you okay? Do you need something for shock?"

"I'm fine," Tamera said, smiling at Tia. "Never felt better. I should go check on my campers," she added, watching the little kids being taken out of their life vests and wrapped in towels.

The way their faces lit up when they saw her coming made her melt inside.

"Tamera! We thought you'd drowned," Rachel said, and promptly burst into tears. Carmen came to hug her, too.

"I told them that there would be an air pocket under the canoe," Oliver said.

Devon gave him a shove. "Shut up, dork face," he said. "You were freaking out, too. I saw you."

"I'm sorry we didn't get to win the race," Tamera said, looking at Devon. "I'm sorry you didn't win your medal."

Devon was staring across at Roxanne. "Canoes don't usually flip, do they?" he asked.

"I don't know. I'm not an expert," Tamera said.

"If someone placed a weight at a strategic part of the hull, then the canoe would flip very easily on a turn," Oliver said thoughtfully.

"What did he say?" Devon demanded.

"I think he meant that someone got at our canoe," Tamera said.

"And I can guess who," Devon said. He glared at Roxanne again.

"There's nothing we can do about it now," Tamera said. "Maybe next time, huh?"

"Yeah, maybe," Devon said. He stomped off down the beach.

Tamera was feeling suddenly shivery. She looked around and saw Roger, also wrapped in a towel, his teeth chattering, and suddenly felt sorry for him.

"How are you doing, Roger?" she asked, sitting beside him.

"Okay, I guess," he said. "Remind me never to drown again. It's not the best feeling."

"You tried to save me, Roger. That was very brave

of you," Tamera said. "And if it makes you feel better, the date's still on."

Roger's face lit up. "Suddenly I'm feeling just fine," he said.

They watched the watermelon-eating contest and then it was time for the counselors' canoe race.

"Aren't you entering?" Roger asked Tamera. "You've got the best muscles in camp."

"No thanks," Tamera said. "I've had enough canoe excitement for one day. I think I'll stick to dry land in the future."

"Too bad. Now you won't have the satisfaction of beating Roxanne," Roger said.

"Let her win. Big deal," Tamera said.

They watched Roxanne get into her canoe. There was a big smile on her face. "Here comes medal number two," she called back to her campers.

The race started. Roxanne's canoe shot ahead of the others. Tamera held her breath. She prayed that one of the other counselors would catch Roxanne, but it didn't seem likely. Then an amazing thing happened. Roxanne kept on paddling, but her canoe stayed where it was. She paddled harder and harder. The canoe didn't move.

Everyone on the beach stood up and started to laugh when they saw the reason why. Someone had tied a rope to the back of the canoe. The other end was tied to a concrete block on the beach. Roxanne wasn't going anywhere. When she realized what was happening, she started yelling and waving her arms.

A second later there was a big splash. Roxanne's canoe had tipped and she had fallen into the water.

All the kids were laughing as she spluttered to the surface.

Tamera looked around and saw Devon and Oliver standing there with angelic expressions on their faces.

"You don't know anything about this, do you?" Tamera asked them.

"I would have done it by myself, but he knew the knots," Devon said.

Oliver grinned sheepishly. "A bowline is the correct knot for tying up boats, I believe," he said.

Tamera put an arm around their shoulders. "That wasn't a very nice thing to do, you guys," she said. "But thanks a million. You're the best."

"And you're not bad either, for a girl," Devon said, grinning at Tamera.

A big smile spread across Tamera's face. Patrick liked her, Tia liked her, Roger liked her, and her kids liked her. This was going to be a great summer.

About the Author

Janet Quin-Harkin has written over fifty books for teenagers, including the best-seller *Ten-Boy Summer*. She is the author of several popular series: TGIF!, Friends, Heartbreak Café, Senior Year, and The Boyfriend Club. She has also written several romances.

Ms. Quin-Harkin lives with her husband in San Rafael, California. She has four children. In addition to writing books, she teaches creative writing at a nearby college.

Sister Sister

COOL IN SCHOOL When Tia joins the Future Female Scientists club at school, Tamera dubs her Queen of the Geeks...until Tia gets to tutor the coolest guy in their class.

YOU READ MY MIND Tia and Tamera have gotten identical answers on their history quiz. Did they read each other's tests? Or did they really read each other's minds?

ONE CRAZY CHRISTMAS Holiday horrors! Tamera's dad has invited his aunt Hattie, his cousin Eliot, and Eliot's bratty son Stevie to spend Christmas at the house. But there are plenty of surprises under the tree....

HOMEGIRL ON THE RANGE Will the twins be split up by a Texas rancher looking to steal Tia's mother's heart?

STAR QUALITY Tamera's playing the lead in Romeo and Juliet. But when fame goes to Tamera's head, she may need Tia to save the day.

HE'S ALL THAT Romance may not be a science, but for Tia it sure can lead to some crazy chemistry.

SUMMER DAZE The twins think they've landed the perfect summer jobs. Dream jobs? Dream on!

ALL RAPPED UP Tia's all rapped up with a senior who's also a rap singer. Is he Mr. Cool or is he just a fool?

by Janet Quin-Harkin

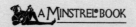
A MINSTREL BOOK

1374